TEARS OF THE HEART

A Western Story

by

LAURAN PAINE

Five Star Western
Thorndike, Maine

A Five Star Western published in conjunction with Golden West Literary Agency.

November 1995

First Edition

Five Star Standard Print Western Series.

The text of this edition is unabridged.

Set in 13 pt. News Plantin.

Printed in the United States on permanent paper.

Library of Congress Cataloging in Publication Data

Paine, Lauran.
Tears of the heart : a Western story / by Lauran Paine.
p. cm.
ISBN 0-7862-0511-3 (hc : alk. paper)
I. Title.
PS3566.A34T43 1995
813′.54—dc20 95-21746

TEARS OF THE HEART

A Western Story

Chapter One

Tie Siding

It wasn't a town. It wasn't even a village. It was a wide place where ties and lengths of steel track were dumped as the railroad followed level ground on its way north toward Fort Laramie.

The track crews were rough, boisterous, hard-drinking men from places like Ireland, Wales, Scotland. There were also Chinese but their camps were apart from Tie Siding, which was just as well; the only thing they had in common with the other track-builders was the variety of back-breaking work that was required to span the West with steel.

Tie Siding had tents, oxen, mules, and some horses. It also had a hutment which was wood to the waist and tenting the rest of the way. It was owned by a man named Mike Farrel, a massive, ruddy-faced individual who parted his hair in the middle, wore pink sleeve garters, chewed Mule Shoe and, it was said, could hit a knothole at fifteen feet when he expectorated.

It was a labor camp of tents, piles of tarred ties, and huge stacks of steel rails. The country southward had been mountainous with twisted cañons. The rail crews were delighted when they broke out of that country; Tie Siding had distant mountains, but where they were now laying track was open country for miles.

There were fights almost every day. Also at night in Farrel's saloon, but big Mike stopped them before any of his back-bar stock was broken. It was expensive bringing liquor north from Fort Collins — by wagon — and the railroad company hauled no freight except its own.

There was a cook shack but mostly the men ate at a tent cafe where the proprietor was a massively muscular red-headed female with pale blue eyes and a mouth like a bear trap. Hard-sweating men had tried to blindside her every day since Tie Siding had been established. The ones who would not listen when she said "No!" were either knocked senseless or chased through camp by the big woman waving a fifteen-inch Bowie knife.

She wasn't pretty, probably hadn't been pretty as a baby, but she could make buffalo hump and gummer cow taste like something created by a Waldorf chef. Her name was Molly Malloy. Unlike the other Irish, she had no "auld sod" accent for an excellent reason: she had been born and raised in the tenderloin of New York City.

Many of the laborers were young men, strong as oxen, hard-living, hard-working. But not all. There were older men, individuals of prime middle age, powerful, not as ornery and noisy as the younger men. Several, it was rumored, were former Confederates. Only one of those seasoned laborers kept the faith. The younger men called him "Old Buttons." Men his own age just said "Buttons." The reason was obvious. Each of his two shirts had Confederacy buttons where other shirts had horn buttons.

But only once did one of the younger men tease him about wearing those buttons of a lost cause. He awakened six hours later with a broken jaw. Because he could not work, the company paid him off; he left Tie Siding and no one ever made another remark about Buttons's lost cause.

The foreman was a massive man, slightly less than average height whose neck and head were the same size. His name was Otto Sheuermann. The paymaster never wrote it the same way twice until the day his exasperation got the better of him. After that he spelled it "Sherman."

On those occasions when the foreman rode the reverse train back to Fort Collins, occasionally as far back as Denver, straw bosses ruled the workmen. Sheuermann was rough but not overbearing. His straw bosses invariably were. Some men just simply are not meant to be bosses. There were fights when Sheuermann was gone. When he returned with mail and supplies, the laborers gathered at Farrel's saloon hoping for letters. Most of the men got them; among those who never did was Old Buttons. He kept his back to those who were handed letters, drank slowly, and avoided looking at himself in the back-bar mirror.

Sheuermann occasionally brought new men. The turnover was not great, but over the months men quit and had to be replaced.

Sheuermann brought back four boys, none over eighteen and at least two were much younger. They would work as water boys, roustabouts, hostlers. They were paid starvation wages but, with neither the muscle nor the experience for anything better, any pay was better than living out of trash bins.

One lad was over six feet tall. He ordered the other boys about, which did not set well with them. All were cast-offs, orphans or, as with the one called Toby, runaways. Toby had been abandoned at a Methodist church doorway. He had been given to the church school. His existence had not been bad, just boringly monotonous. He had run away. He was fourteen years old at the time and knew no other name than Toby. He had asked the school people who his parents had been. They had refused to say and, since everyone had two names, he decided to call himself Lincoln, a good name with most folks but not all. Old Buttons for one did not cotton to anyone named Lincoln.

Toby was growing like a weed; he was gaining height but not muscle. He had brown hair, blue eyes, and even features which suggested that later in life he would be a moderately handsome man.

Saturday nights at Tie Siding were commonly spent at Farrel's hutment-saloon. Because there was no other place for workers to relax, what amusements there were had to be thought up on the ground. Gambling was popular, as was drinking until men couldn't find their rears using both hands; fighting offered a diversion — but not inside the saloon — and betting on just about anything from the possibility of rain by a certain date to how much farther it was to Fort Laramie by newly-laid track. Otto Sheuermann came up with a novel idea: make the boys fight. The winner was to get half a dollar.

Several men went to find the lads and fetch them to the saloon where, amid a rather dense cloud of tobacco smoke and considerable arguing, it was decided that two of the youngest boys should fight first, saving the larger lad, a bully by nature, and the lad called Toby to fight last.

The saloon's furniture was moved out of the way; men called bets back and forth; the room was packed. As word spread more men arrived. Mike Farrel did a land-office business this particular evening. He beamed.

The two younger boys were about evenly matched. At fourteen they were quick, but thin and inexperienced. They fought; men yelled encouragement and advice, which the boys did not hear as they circled and feinted. One was slightly heavier than the other lad. He did not rise up on his toes; he stalked his adversary in a flat-footed, stolid manner.

The other youth, only half grown, wiry and fast, had tears on both cheeks. He was not by nature a fighter. He was a gentle, quiet boy. Each time he'd back-peddle, someone in the noisy crowd would push him forward.

He took a fair beating; his lips had been split; blood ran down his soiled, over-sized shirt. His adversary had not wanted to fight either but, after first blood, he stalked his opponent. He knocked the other youngster down. Rough hands yanked him back upright. He tried sluggishly to avoid the next blow, failed, and went down again, this time with one eye watering and puffy.

Again yelling men wrenched him to his feet and roughly shoved him at his opponent. He could only see out of one eye. He tried to duck under a flurry of blows, was hit solidly on his blind side, and went down again. He was crying; the old shirt was soggy with blood; he raised both fists when a burly man stepped between the lads, shoved the oncoming boy away, turned to the badly beaten youngster and started to herd him through the crowd. For a long moment there was no reaction, then it came, curses, threats, howled complaints, until Old Buttons turned to face the angry men, shoved the lad behind him and waited.

No one attacked.

He gave the lad a dime, told him to go to the cafe, tell the big woman down there Buttons had sent him, and ask her to clean him up.

The lad was glad to escape.

The second pair of fighters were roughly shoved at each other. The larger boy, the natural bully, sneered at the slighter Toby. He swore at him. The crowd roared its approval. Betting on this fight was heavy; bigger amounts were offered in favor of the larger lad.

Toby had seen the first fight. He moved a lot to avoid the large fists of his opponent. Once, too close to the onlookers, a pipe-smoking, red-faced man seized him from behind, propelled him toward his opponent and the noise increased as men called Toby a coward, told him to fight like a man.

He got below two wild blows, raised up too soon, and had half his wind knocked out. He moved, sucked air, and circled. The crowd swore at him, stamped feet, and hooted.

The larger boy stalked Toby, arms high, fists poised; he was wearing a death's-head smile. Toby's tactical retreat was abruptly blocked by the front of Farrel's bar. He had only a moment to decide which way to sidle, left or right. In both directions stamping, yelling, sweaty men were yelling for the larger boy to finish it.

He did. Toby started to move to his right. Otto Sheuermann shoved out a thick arm, stopped Toby in mid-stride, and pushed him back. The larger boy hit Toby twice, once in the ribs and again above the ear on the left side. Toby went down. Sheuermann leaned, grabbed both shoulders, and hoisted Toby to his feet. The moment he was released Toby slid down the bar-front. Men yelled, encouraging the foreman, who leaned to raise the unconscious boy the second time. This time, as he released Toby, someone spun him with a powerful left hand, hit him so hard with the other hand Sheuermann's cigar flew half way to the door, and he fell backwards as limp as a sack of grain.

The saloon became very quiet. Mike Farrel, who kept an ash wagon-spoke under his bar, had it in hand. Old Buttons raised the beaten lad who was too dazed to do more than remain upright. Moving through an opening conveniently provided by the crowd, he led the lad out into the chilly night, sat him on half a whiskey barrel that served as a bench out front, and shook his head as he lighted a cigar.

Later, he took Toby to the big woman named Molly Malloy who had the other lad he'd sent her bedded down in the storeroom, loudly sniffling because men didn't cry.

She looked from Old Buttons to the lad with him and rolled her eyes. She sat Toby in a chair. Before examining him she turned on Old Buttons. "An' you got the nerve to say Indians is savages! You'n your kind are the offshoots of hell! Makin' these boys fight so's you can watch 'em get hurt an' make bets!"

Old Buttons had no smoke rising from his cigar. He watched the woman examine Toby without saying a word. Not even when the lad told her he felt all right, except that his side hurt and Mr. Buttons had saved him from worse.

She did not look around at Buttons when she said, "What's your name?"

"Toby, ma'am."

"Toby, have nothin' to do with the gutter sweepings in this camp. They're the scrapings of hell. Son, you're not built for bare-knuckle fightin'. Don't let 'em dragoon you again. If they try, you run for it . . . come back here to the eatery."

Toby got out of the chair and winced. His side hurt more than he'd admitted. He said, "Yes'm, an' I'm obliged to you."

Molly still ignored Old Buttons as she herded Toby toward the storeroom. After she closed the door, she faced Buttons, still with a high temper. "Makin' children fight! For two bits I'd get Mister Sheuermann to beat the whey out of you. Get out of my eatery an' don't never come back! *Get out!*"

Buttons left the cafe, paused to relight his stub of a cigar, shook his head and wandered down to the corral where another former Secesh was hanging some gray clothing to dry on a rope stretched between a corral post and a sickly little tree. He turned, nodded, and said, "Keepin' clean just ain't possible but it beats itchin'. What was the ruckus at the saloon?"

Buttons sat down on a horseshoe keg, considered the cigar, which was out again, put it back in his mouth to chew the stub, and said, "They made some youngsters fight."

The hostler spat aside, hitched at his britches and wagged his head, but he said nothing. He picked up a worn old towel to wipe his hands and arms. His wash tub was sitting on a fir round. He emptied the water, left the tub wrong side up on the ground, and sat on the round. "I heard Otto tellin' the cook we'd be strikin' camp in a few days an' make our next camp closer to Laramie," he said.

Buttons watched a horse and mule square off over a flake of timothy hay. There would be no fight; mules were only willing to fight when they were cornered; then they used their teeth rather than their heels. He said, "You ever get homesick?"

"Homesick for what? It's all gone, blowed up or burnt down. Carpetbaggers and freed nigras own the South now. There's nothin' to be homesick over. Not any more. I don't want to even think about it, let alone get homesick."

Buttons finally discarded the cigar stub. "How long you worked for the railroad?"

"Two years. Why?"

"Well, one of these days them steel ribbons will fetch

up where them others is buildin' from the west. Then what?"

"Then what? Why, like always, we find somethin' else. I'm gettin' right partial to the West. Lots of room, cheap meat wanderin' around, some real pretty quiet places."

Buttons regarded the other man. "You talk like someone who's fixin' to settle down."

"I might," the hostler said a little defensively. "You'n me . . . our kind . . . have been wanderin' a long time. Before we get too old we better start over, put all of it behind us an' start over. In this kind of country a man could do it. All's he's got to do is quit wanderin', find a decent piece of land an' settle down."

Buttons smiled. "You're likely right but so far I ain't seen country I'd like to settle in."

The hostler snorted. "How long you been buildin' track?"

"Same as you. Two years, about."

"Then you've seen some good country."

Buttons did not deny that. "Lots of it, but I got no feelin' for settlin' down an' startin' over. . . . Not yet. Maybe someday."

The hostler put a pitying look on his friend. "We're not gettin' younger, Buttons. Don't put it off too long. . . . I got to set out the rolled barley for tomorrow."

"How many head?"

"Twenty-four."

Buttons stood up. "I'll help you."

Chapter Two

A Time of Change

Most years springtime came shyly with little warm winds to encourage new-growth grass, small buds on trees, miles-long Vs of geese heading south, hair on horses and cattle beginning to slip, the ground beckoning so that men could come out of hibernation.

The Laramie plains seemed endless under a magnificent canopy of turquoise blue. Homesteaders, a rugged no-nonsense breed, oiled harness, cuffed twelve-hundred pound harness horses, waited for topsoil to dry enough so that it wouldn't ball-up on plow shears. Then nature turned capricious, something which pleased cynics who never trusted her.

It rained for six days straight followed by a bitter wind that chilled men to the bone no matter how much wool they piled on, and everything came to a standstill.

Old Buttons holed up in his tent, waiting for the canvas to be torn loose from its pegs. There was almost no traffic, two-legged or four-legged.

A mile northwest of the camp a homesteader named Nottau, a block-built Dutchman, stood grimly behind a shaking window cursing the wind and rain. His animals stood on the lee side of a shed some distance from his yard, heads down, rumps to the wind, tails splayed, and eyes closed.

He turned back toward the stove with a snarl for the pregnant wife who offered him hot coffee. If he hadn't left the window, he'd have seen something which had been becoming increasingly rare over the years, a straggling band of blanket Indians astride bony nags bucking the wind as they rode in hunched discomfort.

Toby saw them from the loft of Nottau's hay shed, his home for the last few months. He saw something else. One of the squaws was leading a weak, staggering, tall colt. It was not heavy enough to buck the wind. The squaw struck it across the face several times. It pulled back each time she hit it. A buck saw this and turned in beside the colt, swung a war club high overhand. The colt went down in a sprawl. The buck yelled; the woman cast off the lead rope, and both Indians rode on without looking back.

Toby had one old ragged shirt and a pair of someone's cast-off trousers which he'd cut off at the bottom. They were gathered around his middle by a length of cotton rope.

The hay shed groaned in the wind but he'd been burrowing into last year's hay for warmth since before the rains. He had a greasy cloth to keep hay off his food scraps. He had seen the homesteader working in his yard and had expected to have to find another place to live — until the rains came.

Now, he saw the Indians, saw the emaciated colt, felt a distinct pain in the chest when the Indian knocked the colt senseless. As he watched, the colt raised its head, struggled to rise, and fell back.

Toby knew what pain and abandonment were. He knew about going hungry and being scorned. The second time the colt tried to rise, Toby left the shed, leaned into the wind, knelt beside the colt, saw blood where the club had cut an ear, saw the colt's large brown eye on him, and cried.

The wind eased up for a long moment while Toby removed his cotton belt, fashioned a make-shift bridle, pitted all his strength when the colt again struggled to rise, and steadied it when it got up. The wind returned. The colt would have balked at walking against the wind but Toby pulled it. They reached the shed, got inside; the colt smelled hay and made a pitiful effort to find it.

Toby climbed to the loft, pitched down two arm loads. It was old hay with dust and mouse tracks in it. Other horses would not have eaten it, but the colt stood spraddle-legged and did not raise its head for a long time.

There was a swelling on its poll and the torn ear showed drying blood. Toby used a wooden bucket that leaked badly to bring water which the colt did not drink. The water leaked away. Toby sat on a grain barrel which hadn't had feed in it for a long time, watching the young animal.

The wind became fitful as dusk approached. Toby pitched down another arm load of hay. This time the colt folded its legs and went down atop the hay. It watched everything Toby did, not warily as most young horses would have done, but with a resigned attitude.

Toby bedded down in the loft once the young horse flopped over on its side and slept. He awakened several times to peer through the loft-hole but the colt, which he could only barely make out in darkness, was breathing evenly.

Some time during the night the wind stopped. Just after sunrise it returned. It did not blow from the north, as it usually did; it blew from different directions. It was the kind of wind that wore down people who had to be out in it. They braced against it in one direction only to have it change and hit them from another direction. It required no more than a couple of hours bucking that kind of weather to make people as weary as though they had done eight hours of manual labor.

The shed creaked and groaned. Wind came through warped siding, but the colt ate, finally drank water, even began nosing around until it pushed the empty grain barrel over. Toby found an old wheat-straw brush and curried it. The colt did not move but it kept one eye on the boy.

He guessed it to be between one and two years old. It was scarred in many places. One wound, on the near side hind leg, had proud flesh in it. Toby gave it a name: Buttercup. It was the time of year for wildflowers to be sprouting. It was a filly, so he'd named her appropriately.

The Laramie country was noted for wind but, like every other season, it came and went. However, this spring the wind did not slacken for several weeks. It favored homesteaders by drying the top six inches of ground, but they cursed it anyway. The growing season in Colorado and Wyoming was short at best.

Toby stole into Tie Siding after dark to scavenge for food scraps. Once he hit a jackpot. He was rummaging in the trash barrel behind the eatery and got caught when the muscular big woman came out back and saw him.

She did not say a word, just herded him inside, turned up a lamp, studied him, set her back to him and made up a bundle of food which she tied in a gingham napkin and gave it to him. As she did this she seemed accidentally to bump his ribs on the right side. He winced. She said, "Where do you live?"

He hung fire before answering. "In a hay shed a ways from town." His eyes brightened. "I got a horse."

Molly Malloy sat down. "Have you?"

"Some Indians went by. One of 'em hit her over the head because she didn't lead good. I got her inside the shed. As soon as she's real strong, I'll ride her."

"To where?" the woman asked.

Again Toby had no immediate answer. "Somewhere. We'll just keep goin'. I'll find work, get a place to keep her an' buy feed."

The woman sat a long time without expression. When she finally arose, she briefly left the room, returned and put a silver dollar in Toby's hand. Toby stared at it through watery eyes.

He made his way against the wind back to the shed. The colt nickered when he came in. He groped through darkness, put both arms around her neck. She nuzzled him.

He pitched down some more of the old dusty hay, hid the bundle of food, and slept until dawn. He lay in his hay-burrow listening to the wind and holding up the silver dollar so dawn light reflected off it through cracks in the old shed's wall until the colt nickered; then he climbed down, filled the bucket for her, and was surprised that the bucket scarcely leaked at all.

Twice he saw the homesteader go to his barn. He saw the pregnant woman go more often to collect eggs and to milk a gentle old horned cow. Otherwise, although the man's disposition worsened as days passed and there was no slackening of the wind, Toby and his colt lived well in their distant shed, Toby being careful not to be seen from the Nottau house or yard, and Buttercup contented to eat, drink water, and sleep. Her torn ear healed; her eyes brightened, particularly when Toby cuffed and fed her. Even, once, when he climbed onto her back. That time she raised her head in surprise, then went back to eating.

He talked to her, told her all he could about himself. Told her that someday he'd get a job to take care of her, maybe find a good pasture and turn her loose to stand in the shade, get fat, and later, if she wanted a colt, he would find a way to take care of that too because everything needed something to love and protect.

Once, when he went to Tie Siding, he met Buttons. The man took him to the cafe, sat him on a bench, and gently pushed his right side. The pain was instant but less than it had been. He and Molly exchanged a look across the counter. Buttons said, "Healing slow but right."

Molly fed them both even though the eatery had been closed for several hours. None of them talked much but after Toby had finished eating he told them about Buttercup, how she was 'on the mend,' knew him and nickered, had a good, gentle eye. When the woman brought a second slice of rhubarb pie and Toby concentrated on it, she and Buttons exchanged a long look over his head. She disappeared briefly and returned with a pair of new store-bought trousers and a butternut shirt.

The trousers were a tad short and the shirt fit fine except for the sleeves; they too were a little short. Toby put his arms around the woman, hugged her until he had fought back the tears, then he hugged Buttons, whose discomfort was obvious enough to make Molly smile.

After Toby left to buck wind all the way back to the shed, Buttons accepted a cup of coffee, sat a moment gazing into it, then wagged his head. "Men shake hands," he said into the coffee.

Molly smiled. "He's just a child, Buttons."

"Dang near as tall as I am, Molly."

She changed the subject. "What can he do with a colt?"

"I got no idea. Ride it away, he told me." Buttons raised his face. "That shed belongs to a feller named Nottau, a cranky, disagreeable squatter. His wife's younger'n him by some years. She's pooched out with child like a watermelon. He makes her milk a cow when she can't hardly sit on the stool."

"Do you know him?"

"Well, he comes to camp when she's got eggs to sell."

Molly's face brightened. "The egg woman. I didn't know her name. I've bought eggs off her for some time, an' you're right, she's bigger'n a barrel."

Buttons arose to depart. "I'm obliged for the coffee, Molly. If I had a way to do it, I'd take the boy in. I know what it's like to be an orphan. Big enough to shoulder a musket and young enough to cry."

After Buttons had been let out, Molly locked the door and — for the second time that night — took the lamp to her room off the kitchen and sat in a rocking chair until she went to bed. Everyone, she told herself, knows how to cry. The difference between folks is that as men age they develop a shield as hard as oak. In fact, she told herself, in most ways men were as thick as oak.

The wind rattled her only window, the same wind that battered Buttons's tent. The same wind Toby braced into all the way back to the shed, proud in his new pants and shirt. He showed them to the colt who watched Toby turn around and back, patiently waiting to be fed.

The wind began to slacken. It was still capable of keeping folks pretty much indoors, but house-bound homesteaders bucked it wearing coats, hats, and scarves. They had to break ground, work the soil. The weakening force of the wind presaged a cessation altogether; it was a good idea to buck it for a few days in order to have a head start with the farming.

Toby saw the homesteader drive two big pudding-footed horses into the field dragging a plow. He watched as the first earth was rolled over, rich, dark, and moist. He watched through a crack in the siding and had a bad premonition. Not for himself. He'd missed a lot of meals, but so had others. He worried about his colt. It was a certainty that soon now the homesteader would come to the hay shed. Toby's anxieties piled up. They had to leave and soon. He talked to Buttercup, fed her, and impatiently awaited dusk so he could slip down to the railroad camp where he had two friends. Only two. The laborers would have nothing to do with him for not doing better in the fight at the saloon.

The wind died completely after sundown. Toby made good time reaching Tie Siding. He found Buttons out front of the eatery smoking a rough-looking, stubbly little pipe. The cafe was dark. They went to a bench across the road near a long, deep, wooden trough that leaked, sat down, and Toby did not stop talking for five full minutes.

Buttons trickled smoke, gazing over at the eatery. When Toby became silent, the older man leaned forward, knocked dottle from the pipe, and sighed. "What are you figurin' to do?" he asked.

Toby sat slumped. "I don't know."

"You still got that dollar Molly gave you?"

"Yes."

"You could maybe sell the colt for another dollar or two. That'd set you up to ride a stage somewhere . . . to a big town where they use young fellers dungin' out barns, runnin' errands an' all."

Toby faced the older man. "I can't part with Buttercup . . . ever."

Buttons gazed across the road. "Is she broke to ride?"

"I clum onto her back a few times."

"You got a bridle? You got to have somethin' to rein her with."

"I got some cotton rope."

Buttons slapped both legs and shot up to his feet. "Come along. I'll show you how to make a rope bridle. Folks call 'em squaw bridles."

Buttons's tent had a foot locker of some kind kept closed with a large bronze padlock. Otherwise there were two stools, a table with one short leg, some soiled clothing in a bucket, and a steel cot. The lantern hung from a center pole. Buttons turned it up, rummaged until he found a length of rope, pushed his hat back, motioned for Toby to sit opposite him, and said, "Now mind what I'm doin'."

He looped the rope twice, pulled the first loop through the second loop, undid it and motioned for Toby to imitate what he had done.

Toby did exactly as Buttons had done. The older man smiled. "You learn fast. Now then, you do that again. . . . Fine. Now pull that rope through as long as your arm. Good. Now that's your reins."

Buttons leaned on the table. "You'll have to squaw rein her because she won't know how to turn left or right, so you take a length of that rein in each hand, pull to the right an' the left. There's one thing, Toby. If she bucks, a squaw bridle ain't worth a damn . . . unless you see her fixin' to bog her head. A horse can't buck unless it gets its head down. Skinny as you are, I don't know whether you can yank her head up or not. But if she. . . ."

"She won't buck," Toby said.

Buttons sat gazing at the youth in a long silence before saying, "You can make a bridle for her mouth out of one of the loops, but I'd say, don't do it. Colts don't like things in their mouths. Anyway, if she balances it between her grinders, she can break the rope. Now, that slack rope, before you get on her, tuck that in your belt. If she throws you, you'll still have enough rope at hand to yank her head around an' stop her." Buttons smiled slightly. "Now, you got all that?"

"Yes sir. Rope in belt, grab onto it if she dumps me."

Buttons stood up. In the tent he looked larger and thicker. He was in fact a muscular man, hard as stone and tough as rawhide. He went to the foot locker, opened it, took something out, re-locked the chest, returned to the table, and held out his palm.

Toby looked and said, "What is it?"

"It's a Confederate hundred dollar note. Not worth a damn and mostly never was, but it don't take up much space an' maybe someday, some place, you'll take it out an' remember me."

They parted outside the tent. Buttons watched the gangling youth with the rope over his shoulder disappear in the night.

He went down to Farrel's place, ordered a whiskey, and held it so long in his hand the liquid got warm. Mike Farrel came along to say, "Sheuermann's passed word for strikin' camp tomorrow to move up to rail's end and set up again."

Buttons nodded. This had been happening for the full length of time he'd been with the rail gang — build several miles of track, then move up to rail's end, make another camp, and lay more track.

Mike faintly frowned when he said, "You goin' to drink that or let it evaporate?"

Buttons downed the jolt, blew out a flammable breath,

and said, "Are you goin' to set up again yonder?"

Farrel leaned on the bar. "I'll tell you, Buttons, I been settin' up, tearin' down, movin' ever since I commenced servin' the crews south of Denver. I don't know. I'm sick of movin' every month or so. I think Molly's got the right idea. She's movin' back down to that place we passed called Virginia Dale. It's not much but they don't have an eatery."

"You too, Mike?"

"No. I'll go farther south. To make a livin' in my business the closer you can get to a town the better off you'll be."

"Denver?" Buttons asked.

"I was thinkin' farther south. Down near the Colorado-New Messico line. It don't have winters like they got up here. That's another thing. My bones never ached years back, but they do now. Buttons, the winters up here is too long an' too cold."

Buttons pushed the glass forward for a refill, gazed at himself in the back-bar mirror, sighed, and wagged his head. He'd miss the saloonman. Most of all he'd miss big Molly Malloy. Maybe his friend, the hostler, was right. If a man didn't want to spend all his life saying good-bye to people and things, he should settle down; but, as Mike had said, not where it snows hip-pocket high on a tall Indian and winters last an even six months, sometimes seven months.

Mike came back with the drink but had no time for further conversation; men were lined up along the bar. The impatient ones were banging the bartop with their glasses.

Buttons returned to the night, which was so still he could almost hear his heart beating. He crossed to the bench near the leaky trough and fired up his pipe. For a fact he was as gray as a badger; the carnage of scores of battles were receding slightly. He smoked and not for the first time felt lonely — apart from things that had once mattered. A different kind of loneliness.

Across the road the eatery was dark. Molly would be leaving. He would miss her. He would miss the abandoned kid. If things had worked differently, he could have had a boy of his own.

He shook out of that thought. What could he do for a youngster? He had no trade but the one he had been working at for two years, had no particular skill except for marksmanship for which there was no demand and he wouldn't go back to it anyway.

He knocked the pipe empty, arose, and walked back to his tent, and got a surprise. Otto Sheuermann was waiting. The foreman was noted for two things: one, an accent you could cut with a knife, and two, the kind of disposition that brooded. He did not acknowledge Buttons's nod; he stood wide-legged and said, "We're going to strike camp tomorrow. You're not going with us. You're fired."

Buttons was told that about the same time Toby was approaching the shed. It was dark inside. The colt didn't nicker; in fact he could dimly make her out lying on the hay. Horses, when they were healthy, slept standing up. He knew that much as he approached and knelt to put a hand on her. She did not respond as she usually did. He ran his hand up her neck and down to her muzzle, which was soft as silk. The hand got wet.

For five seconds Toby did not move. He lifted the hand which was covered with something sticky and dark. He put the other hand up to her face, felt scorched hair, felt the hole, and brought that hand to his face, too. It was also bloody.

He felt her forehead, traced out the hole amid the scorched hair.

Buttercup was dead. She had been shot!

Chapter Three

Leaving

Buttons helped Molly load her wagon. The hardest part was dismantling the iron cook-stove, carrying it to the wagon and hoisting it over the tailgate. She asked if he was going north with the crew. He told her what Sheuermann had said. She put both hands on ample hips and glared. She had always been careful not to swear where the men could hear her; she had an idea that a woman who swore in front of men would put herself in a position where men would swear in front of her, and men's profanity was different.

But as she stood, hands on hips, she said, "That sauerkraut-eating son-of-a-bitch!"

Buttons was shocked, reddened, and turned aside to lift two boxes and put them in the wagon. Molly would not meet his gaze until she was ready to mount the rig and pick up the lines. Then she beckoned him close, leaned down, and hurriedly kissed him on the cheek. This time Molly was red as a beet; she evened-up the lines, sat poised to move out for a moment before looking down. "Look after the boy, Buttons. Take him with you." She slapped the lines, the rig moved out. Molly did not look back but Buttons watched until she was half a mile down the road. He might have watched longer but his friend, the hostler, came along and said, "You better take down the tent. The flat-car'll be along to move us directly."

Buttons nodded, went in the direction of the tent — which belonged to the railroad company — and worked doggedly moving his personal things outside, helped halter the animals, waited until the flat-car approached in reverse, then avoided a lot of explaining by walking. It was a beautiful day, larks were in the grass, tiny lavender alfileria flowers were underfoot, sod-busters were plowing dark, moist soil; there was heat in the day and mountains hazed by heat in several directions.

When he reached the Nottau place, the woman as big as a swollen toad shaded her eyes and pointed out where a man was walking unevenly in the middle distance. She told Buttons she knew nothing about a boy named Toby. She was clearly uncomfortable in his presence. She pointed several times. "He might know," she said. "That's my husband. I can't help you, Mister."

A man plowed with one foot on solid ground, the other foot in the furrow. From a distance it looked like he had one leg shorter than the other leg. By the time the plowman saw Buttons approaching, he was near to the point where he would jerk the plow and set it for the next quarter mile. It was customary for plowmen to rest briefly before starting the next furrow.

The Dutchman saw a man approaching, removed the lines, and leaned on the plow. He was roughly the same thick build as the stranger, with a bitter downward curve to a nearly lipless mouth. When Buttons got close enough to speak, he had already made his appraisal. Nottau was a man without humor, one of those no-nonsense settlers who resented the fates which had put him on the frontier, disliked humanity, and worked hard to scratch out a living.

They nodded at each other. Buttons did not comment

on the good weather or the promise of a bountiful crop, the ordinary methods countrymen used in greeting each other. He said, "I'm looking for a lad called Toby."

Nottau did not wait for more. "Are you? Well, let me tell you, that worthless bastard lived in my feed barn. I got no idea for how long, but he used up a considerable amount of hay. An' he had a damned runt of a colt in there. Fed it my hay, never come to the house'n asked if he could live in the shed. Never come to ask if he could work for hay. Just snuck in there with that worthless horse an' lived off me."

"Where is he?" Buttons asked.

"I don't know, but I can tell you he won't steal hay for that worthless horse again . . . I shot it."

Buttons was silent for a long time. "The lad . . . did you see him?"

"No. If he's kin to you, Mister, someone owes me for the hay."

Buttons considered the resting big horses, the distant shed, the bitter-faced man in front of him and said nothing. Nottau did though, "I figure he stole maybe a half ton of hay. That'd be worth about a dollar an' a half. You his kin?"

Buttons stood gauging the other man for a moment before turning on his heel and walking back the way he had come. Nottau called after him. "You owe me for the hay."

Buttons did not stop walking until he was close enough to see men loading the flat-car. He sat under a tree, filled his pipe with coarse shag, and smoked in shade until the flat-car pulled out.

Where Tie Siding had been, there were scars to show that a settlement had once been there, a refuse dump, trampled earth, pieces of discarded tin and wood, some left-behind fire wood in little piles, some outhouses left standing. Between morning and afternoon Tie Siding had gone. Farrel's half-wood hutment remained but its tent top was gone. Molly's similar hutment showed four wooden walls three feet high with no canvas top.

He knocked the pipe empty, went down where he'd left his belongings, and considered the silent, empty countryside. It would be a long walk to find a homesteader who would bring a team and wagon to take his things away. To where?

Molly had gone down to the Virginia Dale settlement. He was tempted but abandoned the idea. She would make out; stages stopped at Virginia Dale; people had to eat. He couldn't cook. He had no trade.

He considered the countryside. Somewhere there was a homesteader with a rig he'd hire out. Buttons started walking.

Toby hadn't walked; he had run until he could not run another step, then fell in the grass crying, beating the ground with both fists.

He lay there until near evening then started walking again. The land dwarfed him to ant-size in an immense ocean of grass, sometimes rolling, other times as flat as the palm of his hand, but always with dark-screened mountains in every direction.

He found an abandoned varmint den, crawled inside, and slept until sunup. He hadn't gone a half mile from the den when the fleas started biting. He found a little warm-water meandering creek bordered by willows with pale new leaves and shade.

He stripped and lay in the water, scattering trout-minnows in all directions. That took care of the fleas on his body but later, when he dried off and dressed, there were still enough to take his mind off other things — for a while.

Hunger arrived too, but not until close to evening when he had in sight a set of ranch buildings half hidden in a swale. The builder had chosen the site well. The wind would be less annoying where buildings were protected.

He scouted up the buildings atop the easterly rim of the nearest hillock. There was smoke rising from a fire-place and a kitchen stove pipe. There were horses in a large round pole corral. Where the barn stood, there were trees and what appeared to be a good-sized vegetable garden. One building of logs stood a fair distance from other buildings. It was too large for an outhouse; Toby guessed it was for smoking meat — he was wrong. It wasn't a smoke house.

A woman came outside. She was short and stocky with snow-white hair. She shook a rug and returned to the house. A faint breeze blew from the west. Toby caught the scent of cooking. He waited until dusk passed and full night was down before approaching the buildings. The scent of cooking was stronger the closer he got. He passed the barn where corralled horses lined up on the near side to watch him, little ears forward, dark eyes wide with interest.

He had considered going directly to the house, asking for something to eat. He did otherwise, though, from long habit of being chased off, sworn at, or struck.

He stood next to the barn for a long time trying to figure a way to get into the kitchen. He stood there too long. A stealthy shadow came down the west side of the barn as soundlessly as an Indian's.

Something in the back of Toby's mind tried to warn him — too late. When he whirled, two sinewy arms locked around him from behind, lifted him, and slammed him to the ground. Every ounce of waning strength went into resistance but the man was more than his match. He pinned both arms above Toby's head. The man was gray and lined; right now he was as grim as death.

He stared at Toby for a long time, then reared back, freeing the boy's arms. They sat in the dirt regarding each other. The man was not tall, at least six inches shorter than Toby, but he had the strength some wiry older men were gifted with. He finally spoke. "If you're a horse thief, where's your rope?"

Toby was stunned into silence. The man leaned back against the barn. "How old are you, boy?"

That was easy to answer. "Sixteen, an' I wasn't goin' to steal a horse."

"What was you going to do?"

"I haven't et since day before yestiddy. I was goin' to . . . ."

"Get up," the man said as he arose and dusted his britches. When Toby was facing him, the man said, "There's never been a soul come into this yard, red or white, that went away hungry. Come along."

When they entered the house with its aroma of cooked food, the man addressed a short, white-headed woman breaking pole beans into a large pan at the kitchen table. He said, "Look what I found, Amie."

She looked without speaking.

The wiry old man shoved Toby toward the table. "He hasn't eaten since day afore yestiddy."

The woman arose without a word and went toward a big black iron cook-stove. Once there she turned, studied Toby, and asked a question. "Where are you from?"

"Nearest place was a railroad camp called Tie Siding, ma'am."

"Where are your folks?"

"I don't know. They left me at a church school when I was little."

The old man abruptly said, "An' you run away."

"Yes sir."

The woman piled a platter with a glass of milk beside it, then she and the man stood silent as Toby ate. She looked at the man; he winked at her, moved to the opposite side of the table, and said, "We got a son about your age. His name's Harold. What's your name?"

"Toby. Toby . . . Lincoln."

"Toby. You're pretty scrawny for splittin' wood but, if you'd like to stay a while an' do the splittin', we'd be pleased to have you do it."

The woman came to sit at the table beside her husband. "I'm Missus Roberts and this is Mister Roberts."

Toby paused to swallow before speaking. "I can split wood."

He had made a sound judgment of the man, but the woman he was leery of. "Ma'am, I never et a better meal."

She responded quickly. "Ate, Toby. Not 'et.' There's no such word as 'et.' "

Toby blushed and stopped eating. The man nudged his wife. "Leave it be, Amie."

The woman softened her tone when next she spoke. "You can stay in the bunkhouse . . . but mind . . . no lantern nor candle in there. When you're through, Mister Roberts will settle you in."

Mr. Roberts led the way to that log building Toby had thought would be a smoke house. It was an old bunkhouse with initials and names carved on its walls. There were several old, crudely made branding irons on one wall. On another wall hung a pair of moth-eaten angora chaps, called hair pants. Everything about the bunkhouse was old. Upstairs were six bunks, three on each wall, and a window at the north end. There was a big, black Army stove downstairs for heat.

Toby chose the bunk along the west wall close to the window. Mr. Roberts rummaged for blankets, found three that were moth-eaten but serviceable, then eyed Toby from the stairway. "You'll meet Harold tomorrow. I expect you two'll make out fine. He don't like being 'way out here. He says there's nothin' to do. Good night."

Maybe for Harold there wasn't, but for Toby there was. Logs that had been hauled from the mountains had been sawed into rounds. Fortunately they were still green. The wood was mostly red fir with some pine. Dry pine was a pleasure to split and made into size for wood stoves, but dry fir was something else. If it was really dry, an axe bounced back like a rubber ball. Dry fir was split using a maul and a wedge.

Toby met Harold the next morning. Harold was taller than his father and heavier. He was plump with sullen eyes and a pouting mouth. He sat on a fir round in shade and watched Toby work. Their conversation was limited. Toby worked and sucked air. Harold sat, watched, and asked questions, some of which Toby could not answer, others he could and did until Harold stood up near dinner time and said, "I guess you know how to read an' write. Most waifs don't."

That evening after supper Toby was sitting on a bench out back when Mr. Roberts came along, sat down, and said, "Think you can handle it?"

Toby nodded. He was tired and his body ached, particularly the right side where the boy back in Tie Siding had hit him. "Yes, sir, I never split much wood before. Them as don't weigh much split easy."

"That's pine. The other is red fir. Mind splinters from

red fir; you can't see 'em. You'd ought to use gloves."

"I never owned gloves. Mister Roberts, what's a waif?"

Before the old man replied he pulled a pair of riding gloves from a rear pocket. "Use these," he said. "A waif? Where'd you hear that?"

"From Harold."

"A waif is someone who don't have a family."

Toby tried the gloves and surprisingly they fit perfectly. "I'll take good care of 'em an' I'm obliged, Mister Roberts."

The old man leaned back. "Keep 'em. I got another pair," and before Toby could cause embarrassment by thanking him, Roberts said: "Are you any good on horseback?"

For five seconds the lump in his throat prevented Toby from giving an answer but he eventually managed. "I never rode much, Mister Roberts, but if you want I'll try."

Roberts arose; the moon was coming. "There's a creek over behind the barn a ways, if you want to wash the sweat off."

The following day and the day after that Toby bathed in the creek where he met a hen duck with a trailer of miniature ducks following behind their mother in perfect order.

The hen ignored the white-skinned beanpole using her creek. She paddled wide around him, her ducklings following every maneuver she made like tiny, feathered soldiers.

Two men wearing black suspenders, old floppy hats and trousers ragged at the bottoms arrived one blistering hot day, nodded to Toby, drove around where the woodpile was and off-loaded the balance of winter wood for the Robertses, drove around front where Mrs. Roberts paid them, and drove away not having said fifteen words all the time they had been in the yard.

Harold, who ate breakfast late because he did not leave his bed until the sun was well up, came around where Toby was working, eyed the fresh load of logs, and said, "Do you know how to use a cross-cut saw?"

Toby had never operated a cross-cut saw but he had seen others use them a few times. "I don't but I expect I could learn."

Harold replied as he was moving back toward the house. "Then we'll likely keep you until autumn."

Toby was having a difficult time cottoning up to Harold. When they met, he was polite to him but never started a conversation. When Harold started one, it was consistently patronizing.

On an overcast day with the metallic scent of rain in the atmosphere, Mr. Roberts showed Toby the proper way to saddle and bridle a horse, then saddled two other horses and when they were outside the barn he called over to the house.

Harold and his mother came out onto the porch. Mr. Roberts held up the reins to a saddled horse. Harold said something to his mother whose soothing reply reached as far as Toby. "Do it, sweetheart. Your father needs an extra hand."

Harold crossed to the horses, took the reins from his father, pulled the horse closer, and mounted. Toby watched; there, of course, was a proper way to get on a horse. He imitated Harold and Mr. Roberts said, "Start out right, Toby. Never touch the cantle when you mount a horse. Left hand on the horn with the reins in it, the other hand holdin' to this little straggle of hair in front. Go ahead, try it."

Toby mounted without touching the cantle. Harold

glared at him.

The old man led off at a walk. He held to that gait for a mile before boosting his horse over into a lope. Toby watched Harold, whose fleshy body had a jelly-like movement to it, but neither Harold nor his father ever left the saddle seat. Toby watched the old man; his body seem disconnected at the waist. His rear never left the seat while his upper body rocked with the horse.

Toby tried it. It took practice but, by the time they saw their first band of cattle, he was doing passably well.

The old man removed his lariat and draped it around the horn as he said, "Walk. Just walk slow an' easy, otherwise they'll spook and run."

Toby walked his horse beside sullen Harold. They passed twice around the wary cattle before the old man was satisfied and rode in a different direction.

They did that six times before Mr. Roberts said, "We got to be back for supper. Harold's mother don't like folks traipsing in late after she's cooked."

On the way Toby ignored Harold, who had been ignoring Toby since morning. He instead watched Mr. Roberts; the way he held his reins, the amount of slack he left in the reins, how he leaned slightly for the horse to break over into that easy-riding slow lope without using his spurs.

By the time they got back to the yard daylight was fading. Toby copied everything Mr. Roberts did when they cared for the horses. Harold left his animal for his father to care for and went directly to the house.

Roberts took care of the horse without smiling or speaking. Not until they were finished at the barn did he speak as he and Toby headed for the house.

"Toby, you got to understand Harold. He means well. There's times when he don't feel good."

Toby responded quietly. "We get along, Mister Roberts. Thanks for takin' me along today."

The old man looked around. "That's part of the job, Toby."

"Thanks anyway. I learned somethin' about horses today. But why did we just ride around all them cattle?"

"Lookin' for hung-up heifers, cows with broke horns that got maggots in 'em." Roberts smiled and brushed Toby's shoulder. "I'm glad you come along, boy," he said.

There was very little conversation at supper. Harold arose mid-way through and left the room. Toby thought he must be sick; he'd left most of his supper on the plate.

Harold's mother spoke to her husband. "He's unhappy. He wants to go back to boarding school early."

Her husband went on eating without speaking.

Toby felt uncomfortable. He sensed an undercurrent. As soon as he had finished eating and had thanked Amie Roberts, he went behind the barn to bathe in the creek — and watch the mother duck lead her perfectly behaved babies paddling up and down the creek.

Chapter Four

Trouble

Harold was right. Mr. Roberts kept Toby on into the fall of the year. He hired a neighbor lad to cross-cut logs with Toby. His name was Amos and his folks were members of a religious cult which had homesteaded as a group a couple of miles east.

Amos, like Toby, was filling out. He was a good-natured, tow-headed lad, strong as an ox, a good worker and, when Harold was around, did not say ten words. When he and Toby were together making winter wood, they laughed, joked, played tricks on each other.

Only once did Amos ask a personal question. Toby's answer was given plainly. "I got no folks. I'm a waif."

Once, Amos broke the faith of his cult, which held that a body should never speak bad about folks. He confided in Toby that Harold was a fat, spoiled, mean-tempered big baby whose mother wouldn't let him pee without her saying it was all right.

Toby had his own deep-down opinion of Harold; it went something like this: be pleasant to Harold, avoid him if possible, and ignore his consistent, sly insults, mainly because Mr. Roberts was now paying Toby three dollars a month, and for that kind of money a person could put up with a lot.

It took until late October to get all the logs cut into

rounds and split. The day Mr. Roberts paid Amos off, Harold came from the barn, went to the creek where Amos and Toby were cleaning up, and addressed Amos. "How far is it to your squatter camp?"

Amos arose slowly, dried both hands on an old faded bandanna, and replied slowly. "Maybe a mite more'n two miles. Why?"

"Because your horse in the barn is lame, so you'll have to walk." Harold smiled and turned toward the distant house.

Toby's mouth fell open when Amos caught up with Harold, spun him by the shoulder, and said, "There was nothin' wrong with m'horse this mornin'. What'd you do to it?"

Harold's mouth pulled into a slit. "Take your hand off me, you squatter scum!"

Amos hit Harold so hard the Roberts boy went down, clumsily rolled to sit up, turned to brace with both hands to regain his upright position. When he was upright facing Amos, Toby saw the blood. It seemed to come from his nose and mouth. Harold's eyes watered profusely. Amos moved toward him, fists clenched.

Toby had never seen Amos angry. It held him rooted. He couldn't have moved if a wild horse had been pulling him. He waited for the next blow, but Harold abruptly spun away, went screaming in the direction of the house with blood down his shirt-front.

Amos ignored Toby, went to the barn, and by the time Toby arrived Amos was arising from a kneeling position with a thin strand of wire in one hand. He led the horse out. It limped. Amos saddled and bridled it without a word, led it outside, turned it several times until the circulation had improved, then mounted it and glared down at Toby. "My paw'n the others were right. That ain't no man-child they're raisin', it's a lard-bellied, whinin' no good son-of-a-bitch."

Toby was still standing in the doorless wide barn opening watching Amos, who was small in the distance, when Mr. Roberts came up and spoke quietly.

"What happened? Which one of you hit Harold?"

"I didn't, Mister Roberts. Harold lamed-up Amos's horse with a piece of wire, then come to the creek and told him he'd have to lead the horse home."

The old man sat on a small barrel which had been up-ended. He gazed briefly at his work-hardened hands before speaking. "Toby, Harold told his maw you held him so's Amos could hit him. Did you?"

Toby stared. When Harold had gotten hit, Toby was a good twenty feet away.

"Did you, boy?"

"No sir. Amos went after Harold. He was mad. I never saw Amos mad before. Harold was walkin' away. Amos grabbed his shoulder, turned him."

"Hit him?"

"Yes sir."

Mr. Roberts stood up and started away without looking at Toby. He walked all the way back to the house with both hands in his pockets and his head down.

Toby finished up at the creek, went down to the bunkhouse for a comb he had found, and was ready for supper — but dreaded going to the house.

For some inexplicable reason he felt guilty. When he entered the kitchen, Harold's mother did not turn. The table was set for three, not four. Mr. Roberts came in from cleaning up out back, he nodded to Toby, looked at his wife's back, as straight as a ramrod, considered the table and blew out a rough sigh as he said, "Harold ain't comin' to supper, Amie?"

"Yes, Harold will be along, but right now I want that boy off the ranch. *Right now!*"

"Amie, it was the squatter boy, not. . . ."

She flung around, eyes blazing. "Toby could have helped Harold. Those squatters are a worthless, sneaky lot. Toby owed loyalty to the brand he worked for and you know it. I want him out of my house and off this ranch right now!"

"Amie, it's supper time. In thirty years we ain't never sent someone on their way hungry."

The stocky, white-haired woman raised a rigid arm in the direction of the door. "Out! He deliberately stood by and let that squatter rat beat up on Harold. Didn't give him a chance to fight back. He told me how it was. Amos beat on Harold an' that one stood by grinnin'." The rigid arm did not so much as sag. "Off this ranch right now, John Henry Roberts. Out of my house! Off this ranch now. Tonight. This instant. If you won't do it, I will. My paw's hawgleg's still in the commode. Well!"

Toby took the initiative by turning away, walking out into the warm dusk to pause on the porch. Mrs. Roberts hadn't been rational; first she'd said Harold had told her Toby held Harold for Amos to beat on him, then she said Toby had stood by grinning.

Mr. Roberts closed the door softly behind himself and stood beside Toby for a moment before speaking. "I'm sorry, son." He dug in a pocket, produced three silver cartwheels, and handed them to Toby. "I was figurin' to put you on permanent last month. Take it, boy. You earned it."

Toby pocketed the money without speaking. He had just lost something: a place of his own, a bed, a family to eat with, work he took pride in, the possibility of a future on a working ranch.

Everything had crumbled. He turned toward the old man. "Mister Roberts, you got a horse you'd sell for three dollars?"

The old man looked in the direction of the corral. "Let's go see," he said.

Roberts had seventeen horses; mostly he'd pulled their shoes and turned them out. Four were in the corral. A cranky gray mare and three geldings — among horsemen called "horses." Roberts leaned on the top stringer, pointed, and said, "That dark sorrel, the one I rode. I'll get a shank."

Mr. Roberts handed Toby the lead rope, left him standing briefly, went into the barn and returned lugging an old Texas A-fork saddle with loop-through stirrup leathers, a blanket, and a bridle. As the old man rigged out the horse, he said, "Step inside the doorway, Toby, an' fetch that bedroll." When the horse was ready, the old man lashed the bedroll behind the cantle, seemed not to see the lad's outheld hand with four silver dollars on the palm. He said, "Toby, man to man, I'm satisfied you told the truth. You're young. What I got to say you think back on five, ten years from now. Harold's our only child. Good luck, boy. You got the makings of a good man."

Mr. Roberts held out his hand. Toby dropped the four dollars in it. Roberts leaned, shoved the money down the front of Toby's shirt, and smiled. "I'll tell you something else, Toby, I figure in this life a man don't often get the son he'd like to have. You'll get by."

Toby swung into the saddle. There was a lump in his throat as large as a peach pit. He couldn't speak, so he bent with his hand outstretched. Mr. Roberts gripped hard and stood a long time, even after he could no longer see Toby and the sorrel horse. He did not turn away until even the sound of shod hoofs were lost in the darkness.

It was a warm night with a scimitar moon. For Toby it could have been full dark. He did not know where he was going, had a limited knowledge of the country, and let the horse have its head.

Sometimes, he would think back. His sorrel horse was the animal Mr. Roberts rode. He was cow savvy, held a rope, could cut calves away from frantic mammy cows. He was worth at the very least forty dollars.

Toby bedded down beside a willow creek, crawled into the bedroll, and fought back the tears. In another year or so he would be eighteen. Grown men didn't cry.

Two days later, passing through rolling grassland country where pines and firs grew scattered, his heart nearly stopped. An Indian was standing in tree shade watching him. All Toby knew about Indians was that they were treacherous, stole anything not chained down, and killed people.

At this moment he would almost have traded the sorrel horse for a gun. He had to ride past the tree-shaded Indian so he acted as though he had not seen the man. It was hard — especially when he passed the big tree where the Indian was moving to keep from being seen.

Toby made a solemn promise. The first settlement he came to he would buy a gun.

He did not look back for about a mile. When he did, his stomach was still knotted. There was no sign of the Indian. But from that point on he preferred riding the high ground and avoiding stands of trees.

The fourth day, while his horse was picking grass on a postage-stamp meadow, Toby trapped three Dolly Varden trout, made a fire, and cooked them using a fretwork of green limbs. As he was eating, he accepted what instinct told him: a man has to be resourceful, has to figure things.

He emerged from some rough country on the fifth day to sit his horse admiring the open country dappled with distant cattle. There were no buildings in sight but westerly a few miles smoke rose straight up which meant there would be people.

He angled around in that direction, keeping to high ground as much as he could and, when he finally entered a fringe of trees which seemed to separate him from that smoke, he dismounted and led the horse on a prudent reconnaissance. The last thing he wanted was to walk into an Indian camp.

The clearing where the fire smoked was about eight or ten acres in size. There was a log house in the middle and a straggling pair of wagon tracks going from the cabin into a northerly stand of big trees.

Out back was a set of pole corrals where two big horses had caught his scent and were standing inside the corral, heads up, ears pointing.

He considered riding on in. Someone was tending that fire; someone was caring for that pair of big horses. He turned away, got back astride, and remained in the trees on a northward course until even the smoke was hard to discern. He bedded down ahead of sundown upslope from a cold-water creek where he trapped more Dolly Vardens, cooked, and ate them. It had been a hot day and was still warm after the sun sank. He stripped, went down to the creek, where cold water almost stopped his breath, bathed in a hurry, then sat on an ancient rock until he was dry enough to dress and return to the small stone ring he'd made for cooking the fish.

He listened to birds, laid back, and remembered a mother duck and her small look-alikes when he'd bathed in a warm-water creek far south, and what seemed like a long time back.

He had been riding eight days when the land flattened a little; trees were distant; the heat was bearable but shade would have been nice. He hadn't eaten in two days; he endured some things for the best of all reasons — he had no gun to kill meat and there were no creeks that he knew of in the country he was passing through. But there was a settlement. Even from a hill a mile away it looked like a large and thriving place.

He set his course for the cluster of buildings, studied them as he approached, and saw what most likely was the cause of the settlement's thriftiness: newly laid railroad tracks passed along the northeast side of the settlement.

He thought of Buttons; for as long as he lived, railroad tracks would remind him of Tie Siding and Molly, but most of all Old Buttons.

Where he came over the berm onto the north-south roadway, there was a sign. The town was called Bridger and its population was said to be three hundred people.

He reached the livery barn at the lower end of town with the sun reddening as it settled lower. The liveryman was one of those lanky Texans with a prominent Adam's apple and a straggly dragoon mustache stained brown above his upper lip. He leaned on a hay fork watching the youth leading the savvy-looking sorrel horse.

Toby tied the horse to a stud ring, flung up the left stirrup, and was pulling the latigo loose before the lanky, long-faced man put aside his fork and approached. His voice was accented and tinny when he said, "Dime a day, young feller. That's outside in a corral. Stalled is fifteen cents a day." Toby nodded, lifted off the saddle, and headed for the harness room with it. The tall man shagged after him. As Toby was racking the saddle, the liveryman said, "In advance."

Toby brought forth a cartwheel, handed it over, and waited for the change. The liveryman had to dig out a long pocket purse that had to be pushed up from the bottom before coins could be seized. As he laboriously counted the silver into Toby's hand, the tall man scowled. Counting anything, money, marbles, or chalk, was something he did with difficulty. When Toby was pocketing the change, the tall man smiled. "You wouldn't want to peddle me that sorrel would you?"

"No. Him'n me come a long way. We're partners."

The Texan's eyes narrowed slightly. "You ridin' alone, are you?"

"Just me'n my horse."

"Got friends in Bridger. Kinfolk maybe?"

"Nope. Never been here before, don't know anyone."

The Texan's narrowed eyes were fixed on Toby. "Passin' through in a sort of hurry, are you?"

"Not in a hurry, Mister. Saw the town, figured I'd get some grub an' keep goin'."

The liveryman pursed his lips, which gave his face a sly look. "I pay good money for horses like that sorrel."

"Like I said, he ain't for sale," Toby replied.

"Is that a Colorado brand on his left shoulder?"

"Yes. It's the brand of a feller I worked for in Colorado."

The Texan faintly nodded. "An' you got a bill of sale from this feller you worked for?"

"A what?"

"Bill of sale for the horse."

"Mister Roberts gave him to me."

"Is that a fact? Boy, folks don't just up an' give some

kid a horse like that. How old are you?"
"Seventeen."
"An' you got no bill of sale for the sorrel?"
Toby was uncomfortable. "All I know is that Mister Roberts gave me the horse."
"So you got no bill of sale," the liveryman said. "Let's you'n me take a little walk. What'd you say your name was?"
"Toby Lincoln. Walk where?"
"Over to the marshal's office. Boy, that's a right good horse. Folks don't give away horses like that. In Wyomin' horse stealin' is a real serious business."
"I didn't steal him. Mister Roberts gave him. . . ."
The fist was bony, hard as stone, and too fast for Toby to avoid it. He fell against an old desk, dazed, unable to react quickly enough. The second blow sank into his middle, doubling him over. The liveryman yanked him upright, propelled him out into the runway, and punched him over the kidneys from behind as he herded him to the roadway, across it and northward to a solid stone building with one barred roadway window.
He shoved Toby inside. The gray, grizzled man at the table was holding a coffee cup half raised. He looked from Toby to the liveryman. "What you got, Sam?" he asked in a deep, coarse voice.
"A horse thief, Marshal. I got the horse at the barn." The Texan roughly shoved Toby to a wall bench where he crumpled in pain. "He's ridin' a sorrel horse with a Colorado brand, got no bill of sale, said a feller he worked for give him the horse. Charley, go look at that horse. No one gives a horse like that to some raggedy-assed kid with string holdin' his shoes on an' a cotton rope holdin' up his pants."
The marshal put aside the coffee cup, leaned on the

table gazing at Toby. He was a hard-eyed, bull-necked old man with a wound for a mouth. "What's your name, boy?" he growled.

The answer was unsteady. "Toby Lincoln."

"You stole a horse down in Colorado . . . how far south?"

"I don't know. A couple of weeks of ridin'. Like I told the liveryman, Mister Roberts gave me the horse. Him'n me been partners."

"You'n this Mister Roberts?"

"No sir, me'n my sorrel horse."

The man wearing the badge exchanged a long look with the liveryman before arising and taking down a ring of keys from a wall peg behind his table. "All right, Sam. I'll take care of it."

The liveryman had a question. "What about the horse he stole?"

The lawman shrugged. "Public auction, like always."

After the liveryman departed, the marshal herded Toby down a narrow corridor into a strap-steel cage of which his jailhouse had four, two on each side of the narrow passageway. The marshal went over Toby for weapons, found the silver dollars, and took them with him when he locked Toby in and returned to his office.

It was cool in the cell, much cooler than it would be outside. It was also dark except for a sliver of light entering through a high, long, and very narrow slit in the rear wall that had two steel bars set in the stone, an unnecessary precaution; the window was too narrow for anything but maybe a snake to pass through.

Toby was sick to his stomach. He sat on the wall bunk, eventually leaned back but that also hurt. He had no appetite, not after the shellacking he'd taken from the liveryman. He would have slept if he could have, and in fact he did sleep, but not until the small hours of the following day. He hadn't been asleep long when the grizzled town marshal appeared in the passageway with two small canisters which he shoved under the door, scarcely more than glanced in at his prisoner, and returned to his office.

One canister had black coffee in it; the other was two-thirds full of some kind of watery stew.

He ate every drop of the stew and also drained the coffee pail although he had never formed a taste for coffee.

By full daylight he was able to cross his cage and return. His back was still sore but at least with food in it his stomach no longer bothered him.

Chapter Five

An End of Summer

Toby was fed more or less regularly for six days. On the seventh day, which happened to be a Tuesday although Toby did not know it, he was taken in chains to Bridger's judicial chamber, which was a large room above the fire hall furnished with a table, several chairs opposite the table, and three rows of benches. The only ornament in the court room was an American flag whose staff had been pushed into a nail keg full of dirt.

The town marshal growled for Toby to take one of the chairs opposite the table and not to speak unless spoken to. Then the marshal read the charges which were exactly as the liveryman had told him when he'd brought Toby to the jailhouse.

His Honor was a short, pale-eyed old man with a massive gold chain across his vest, which was otherwise decorated with smudges of cigar ash. The judge listened to the charges, put his attention on the prisoner, and spoke roughly.

"Boy, when I was your age stealin' horses was a hangin' offense."

Before His Honor could continue Toby said, "I didn't steal that horse. The man I worked for give him to. . . ."

"Shut up!" the judge yelled. "You interrupt me again, boy, an' I'll send you down the road for five years . . .

I may do that anyway. If there's one thing I got no damned use for, it's a horse thief. You just set there an' keep your mouth shut."

Like many irascible people, once His Honor had exploded it required some time for him to regain his composure. He sat glaring at Toby but when next he spoke he addressed the town marshal. "Have you seen the horse, Charley?"

"Yes, Your Honor. He's in his prime, built real good . . . Sam told me he could sell that horse for maybe fifty, sixty dollars."

"Bill of sale, Charley?"

"No sir, he don't have one."

His Honor returned his hostile gaze to Toby. "I been holdin' court twenty-eight years. In that time a man learns things. One is that a man that'll steal will lie, meanin' a damned horse thief would lie. Now then, I'm in a hurry today, so you give me a reason why you'd steal a horse, an' s'help me Gawd if you lie I'll send you away. Speak up, boy."

Toby hadn't slept well for six days, which might not have mattered but the merciless old man at the table terrified him. "Mister Roberts gave me that horse the night he had to fire me. That's the truth, Judge. He had to let me go because his wife. . . ."

His Honor exploded again, "Marshal! Lock him up until the prison wagon gets here. Boy! I warned you about lyin'. This Roberts feller fired you. You admitted that. An' you was goin' to tell me after firin' you he gave you a good horse. What'd you say his name was, Charley?"

"Accordin' to him it's Toby Lincoln, Your Honor."

The judge arose as he said, "Stand up, Toby Lincoln. I sentence you to two years in the territorial prison."

His Honor remained standing briefly before picking up a dog-eared book, nodding to the marshal, and marching out of the room. At the doorway he lifted out a large gold watch, flipped open the case, swore, pocketed the watch and almost ran down the stairs because the noon stage would be leaving within a few minutes and he had to be on it in order to reach the next town where he was scheduled to hold court.

The marshal scowled. "Stand up, boy. Now walk ahead of me back to the jailhouse. Don't try to run. I can bust your leg with one shot from the road in both directions. *Get up! Now walk!*"

For Toby the ensuing four days were a torment. When he asked the town marshal about the prison, his answer was a callous glare and not a word.

The day the prison wagon arrived there was a driver, a gun guard, and three prisoners inside in irons. While the marshal was getting signatures from the driver for delivery, and Toby was waiting outside with the cold-eyed gun guard, the liveryman came along, nodded to the guard, gave Toby a contemptuous look, and entered the jailhouse. The marshal got his prisoner's receipt and the driver was leaving when the liveryman put a ten dollar greenback on the marshal's desk, lowered his voice and said, "Sold the horse to old Enos Cargill. Got sixty dollars. That's your cut."

Outside, the gun guard prodded Toby around back, unlocked the door, and shoved him inside. Within minutes the rugged, dark wagon with barred, glassless windows on each side, started ahead with a jerk.

It was dark inside. The three other chained prisoners eyed Toby impassively. Two were old men, scarred, weathered, and mean-eyed. The third one was even younger than Toby. His eyes were red. He was thin, had red hair, freckles across the saddle of his nose, and a wide mouth.

The wagon either had no springs or very weak ones. On a washboard road it was like riding a hobbled horse. One of the old men asked what Toby had done. When he answered truthfully, "Nothing," neither of the older men either looked in his direction or spoke to him again.

The youth was different. He was frightened, bedraggled, and scrawny. "I stole two cans of peaches out'n a store. The judge gave me a year for grand theft."

Toby considered the youngster. "Was the judge an old man with a big gold chain across his middle an' a nasty temper?"

The youth nodded. "Yes. His name's Judge Stover. Up north where they held me in jail, a deputy sheriff told me he's the meanest, crankiest judge on the circuit. You didn't steal no horse?"

"No. He was give' to me by a man I worked for down in Colorado."

The youth stuck out a filthy hand. "I'm Abel Sanford."

Toby shook. "Toby Lincoln."

By mid-day it was like an oven inside the wagon. Once, the rig stopped at a way-station to water and grain the horses. The driver and gun guard ate, climbed back to their seat, and drove on.

One of the older men leaned to whisper to the other man, who looked shocked, then leaned to whisper back. As though in reply the first man fished around in back of his rumpled, stained clothing and produced a wicked-bladed knife with a ten inch blade. As he did this he grinned and said, "Dassn't set straight. That thing's got a point on it like a needle."

His companion said, "Put it up," and as this was being done the other man asked a logical question. "How'd you ever get past all them deputies without them findin' that thing?"

"Had it snugged up between m'legs." The speaker glanced at the youths who were regarding them in awe. The man with the knife had bad teeth which showed when he grinned at the boys. "Just mind your manners an' I'll have you out'n here next time they open the door."

The older men spoke softly back and forth. Abel Sanford looked at Toby without speaking. Toby considered the older men. They were bitter-faced, hardened individuals. He wondered how the one with the knife figured he could use that thing against the gun guard and driver who both wore belt-guns and carried sawed-off shotguns.

He could have spared himself the anxiety. About a mile or so down the road in the middle of open country the wagon came to a dead stop, both men from the high seat climbed down, one on the left side, the other one on the right side.

Toby heard them coming around to the back of the wagon, heard one of them fumble with the big bronze padlock without realizing the two older men had scooted down their bench and were next to the door as someone outside flung it open.

No one moved for five seconds. Toby and Abel Sanford seemed unable to breathe. Both the whip and the guard were standing in sunshine beyond the flung-back door holding double-barreled shotguns, both barrels at full cock. The gun guard snarled at the pair of older men. "Climb out." As he said this, the gun guard took several rearward steps as did the whip.

The prisoners climbed out awkwardly; leg irons were like horse-hobbles except that the chain between each steel cuff was longer. It was difficult to climb out of the wagon but both older men managed.

The gun guard aimed his shotgun at the soft parts of the man with the knife and held it stone-steady as he spoke. "What were you goin' to do with that pig-sticker? Throw it on the ground." When the prisoner hesitated, the gun guard swung the steel butt-plate of his scatter-gun upwards. Afterwards Toby thought the guard must have done that many times. The prisoner's chin bled as the man went down, unconscious.

The guard pointed his weapon at the other older man. "Get the knife! Move, you son-of-a-bitch!"

The prisoner moved, groped for the knife, straightened, holding it, and the whip said, "Shoot, Arnie! He's threatenin' you! Kill the worthless bastard."

The gun guard did not shoot; he made a wolfish smile which showed several gold teeth and softly said, "Drop it!"

The prisoner let the wicked-bladed knife fall.

The guard eased down the dogs on his shotgun and used it to gesture with. "Pick him up, dump him back inside, an' Mister, when you're in there, look up. You'll see a little square place closed off from the inside. He'n you ain't the first damned fools who didn't know I could see you from the high seat by liftin' the lid of that hole. Now chuck him inside."

The prisoner had to strain. The unconscious man was dead weight. He shoved him in, climbed in after him and, as the door was locked from the outside, the breathing-hard older man leaned to consider his companion, and viciously kicked him in the ribs.

Toby was sweating rivulets. He knew the whip and gun guard had canteens because he had seen them tossed into the front boot back at Bridger, but he wasn't sure a plea for water might not upset that murderous pair on their high seat.

Abel leaned to help the beaten man sit up. The other older man offered no assistance and glared. The cut chin was still bleeding, not as profusely as before but still trickling when the battered prisoner raised an unsteady hand to assess the damage. His companion on the seat snarled at him. "You damned fool. You could have got us all killed!"

The injured man eventually got back on the seat, leaned forward with a filthy, old, faded blue bandanna held to his injury. Not a word was said until the prison wagon arrived in a fairly large settlement where it was parked behind the jailhouse, the horses taken off to be cared for, and the whip opened the door with two canteens in one hand, a cocked Colt in the other hand. He snarled as he flung the canteens inside.

"You don't get no supper, just breakfast. Sleep tight, you damned vermin."

The heat did not diminish inside the wagon; full darkness was down; the disgruntled older prisoner looked at his companion with the discolored and swollen lower face and said, "If you got any more smart ideas, keep 'em to yourself. We'll be home tomorrow afternoon. When I tell what happened, they're goin' to call you a damned idiot."

Neither Toby nor Abel Sanford slept well. The injured man occasionally groaned but his companion stretched out on the floor and slept like the dead.

Toby was roused by a soft sound outside on the west side of the wagon. He did not move. The sound was like someone in slippers or barefoot might make. He was wide awake when something was tossed through the barred window above and landed in his lap. He sat up, feeling for whatever had come past the window bars. It was a soft bundle wrapped in an old red and white checkered napkin. Before opening it, he could smell food. He nudged Abel. The bundle had several cold fried chicken wings and what felt like about a dozen oatmeal cookies.

He and Abel ate everything including crumbs. The older men did not stir. Except for an occasional groan, the injured prisoner did not move.

When they finished, they tossed the old napkin back through the window. Toby did not want the guard or driver to find it, but shortly after dawn when the horses were being hitched to the pole the gun guard came around back, unlocked the door, opened it and pointed a cocked Colt inside. He held up a greasy red and white napkin — and grinned.

"It's an old widow-woman. She's why we don't feed prisoners at this place. Every wagon she sneaks up and tosses food scraps inside. Her son died on a scaffold six, seven years back." He slammed the door, padlocked it, and answered curtly when the whip asked if he was ready to leave.

"Old Lady Farley done it again."

The morning was crisp, cool, and clear. By mid-day with heat increasing, the pair of older men emptied both canteens. The injured man's efforts at this started his chin bleeding again, but he could talk. Not clearly but adequately when he addressed the other older man. "I'm goin' to kill Blackburn if it's the last thing I ever do."

His companion glanced up at the little closed square in the roof. "It just might be the last thing. Or maybe he'll kill you first."

The driver was taking his time, which suited the prisoners. It was another wash-board stretch of road. When the rig moved along at a trot, it rattled every loose slat and bolt and made sitting on the benches inside not just uncomfortable but difficult.

Toby arose to look out a window. The uninjured older man dryly said, "Don't get anxious, boy. If old Judge Stover sentenced you for horse stealin', my guess is that what you'll see directly will be your home for the next couple of years." The speaker eyed Toby for a moment before also saying, "Two years . . . hell, boy . . . feller your age can do two years without changin' his socks." The speaker turned to his companion with the blood-stiff shirt and the terribly swollen lower face. "How old was you the first time?"

The injured man made no attempt to reply. He was holding the blue cloth to his lower face; it was soaked with water.

The uninjured prisoner, a man at least in his mid forties, arose to lean and also look out the barred window, bracing himself as he did so. Without turning away he addressed the injured man. "You reckon ol' Cranston's still there?" He probably had not expected a reply because he barely allowed time for it before also saying, "I wish I knew how he kept from gettin' hanged. They always hang 'em down here for murder."

A voice spoke from the little covered square in the roof. "He died last year. Some disease that was runnin' through the prison. He was old as dirt anyway."

They all looked up but the little square had been closed.

Abel stood up beside Toby; he had to stand on tip-toe to see out. His voice seemed small when he said, "Is that it? It looks like a fort made of old rocks. Ugly-lookin' place, Toby."

The uninjured man spoke from his resumed seat on the far bench. "You think it's ugly outside . . . wait until you been inside for a while." The man laughed.

There was a settlement about a half mile from the formidable stone prison. It was a sad affair for a settlement. The buildings had been erected without planning; no one painted anything. There was a log church from which the cross had been shot off some years earlier during a contest between the alcoholic constable and two released members of the Plummer gang.

The road passed through and veered left. The closer the wagon got to the prison the farther down Toby's heart sank. He had never been confined, had never thought about being confined, but the closer he got to that massive, tall, ugly structure the more a fear of being held inside for two years frightened him.

There was a massive, steel-reinforced, oaken gate, tall, wide and thick. It required two men to open it. Inside wooden ramps ran completely around the four high walls, manned by sentries in look-alike dark coats and trousers, every one of them carrying — not the customary carbine — but a long-barreled rifle.

They were left to languish inside the wagon after the guard and driver had climbed down amid shouted greetings from the catwalks and elsewhere on their way toward a log building built facing the gates with its back to the southerly rock wall.

The uninjured prisoner leaned to look outside, and said, "Nothing's changed." He twisted to look down at the youths. "I been here three times. My fourth trip will be lucky. I'll be out come next summer."

The injured man spoke almost incomprehensibly. "If you'd backed my play back yonder, we wouldn't neither of us be in again."

His companion turned slowly as someone outside was rattling the hefty old padlock. "You're right, we'd never have been in here again. We'd had our insides scattered all over hell. Two shotguns an' you with that damned knife."

When the door swung open, four men dressed identically stood clear with what Toby thought were axe handles. One man gave an order. "Out."

Another guard with the features of a bull dog smiled at the uninjured older man as he said, "Tracy, we missed you. Welcome back. What happened to your friend?"

Another guard snarled. "Shut up! No talking. Tracy, you know where to go . . . march!"

Chapter Six

The Hand of Fate

The prison was a brutal place where existence was regulated by either whistles or bells, the latter loud, deep-toned; they had been acquired from an Eastern ship supply company. The prison had more guards than prisoners. Toby was to learn this condition fluctuated; more crimes were committed in spring, summer, and fall than in winter.

He and Abel Sanford were put into the same cell where the commode pot hadn't been emptied since the previous prisoner had vacated the cell. Flies were thick and, while fresh air was abundant in the cell with its one little slit of a window, the stench was undiluted.

The prisoners were herded to a large mess hall for meals and herded back, some to cells, others to an exercise yard which during winter was ordinarily under two feet of snow.

Abel became Toby's shadow. One night during sweltering heat a gray, sad-faced old man, a permanent inhabitant and therefore permitted some leeway, stopped in front of the cell looking in. He looked longest at Abel. He asked how old Abel was.

"Fourteen, Mister."

The old man looked scornful. "You're eighteen, boy. You know why? Because they can't put you in here under eighteen. They got to put you in a foundling home." The old man made a death's-head grin. "I've seen 'em come here no more'n twelve. It's easier for the law to say they're eighteen." The old man lingered, pale, watery eyes fixed on the boys. A guard came along, growled something, and the old man shuffled away.

There were work parties. Manual labor was nothing Toby was not accustomed to. He was strong, solidly built, maybe a little tucked-up; but three meals a day, provided for quantity rather than quality, ironed out most of the pleats in his stomach.

Abel ate everything in sight. After six months, with winter past and spring returned, with work details taken out under heavy guard, Abel paired off with Toby. That spring the old man with watery eyes died. All the boys knew was that he stopped appearing. Another man, dark with black eyes, teeth worn down evenly, and an unkempt mass of steel gray hair whose name was Epifanio Salazar, told them during a rest period on a beautiful spring day the old man had murdered his wife and the man he caught her in bed with. He did not say more, did not mention the old man's name because it did not matter.

Salazar was called " 'Pifas," the nickname of anyone whose first name was Epifanio. The guards and other work-party prisoners treated the dark man with respect. One day at supper a weasel-faced man sat down next to Toby and said, " 'Pifas taken a liking to you fellers. He's a good man for a friend. You know what he done two years ago? Him'n another Mexican got into a fight. Before the guards could reach 'em, 'Pifas strangled the other feller." The weasel-faced man winked. "Murder in here ain't the same as outside. Outside they hang you for murder. In here . . . the other Mexican was troublesome; no one had no use for him. In here they just keep you until you die. You know why? They don't want no one on the outside to know murder's been done in here."

Three days later 'Pifas was detailed to crowbar stumps out of springtime soft earth. Toby was strong. He was also savvy. When the three of them could not budge an oak stump and 'Pifas swore in frustration, Toby placed 'Pifas's crowbar over a boulder, positioned his own bar beside it, and told Abel to do the same. When all three of them strained in one place, the stump yielded a little. Without a word Toby re-positioned their bars atop a larger boulder and this time the stump came halfway out of the ground. A bull-necked, red-headed guard who had been watching said, "Once more, lads."

The stump rocked forward leaving a gaping hole. The guard smiled. "You boys is wastin' your time in here. You'd ought to be outside where good sense'd make you rich."

Abel continued to eat like a horse without gaining weight. Toby sheltered him when he could. The younger boy worried him. He became a year older, without growing taller nor increasing his weight. The second winter he developed a cough. A burly guard named Bannion made a point of seeing that Abel went out to cut wood in the snow. When Abel returned, he would drop onto his bunk, red-faced and clearly ill. Once when the sadistic guard came for Abel, Toby volunteered to go in Abel's place. The guard stood wide-legged in the doorway, gazing at Abel on his bunk and shaking his head. "He goes, not you. They got rock-breakin' for you today."

Toby faced the guard who was holding his club in both hands. "He's sick," he said.

The guard again shook his head. "Sick, hell. He's been doin' less'n less for a long time. Abel, get up."

When the younger boy rolled to the edge of his cot, braced with both hands to shove upright, the guard snarled at him. "Don't play-act with me. I been handlin' malingerers like you a long time. I know a lazy bastard when I see one. *Stand up!*"

Abel got to his feet, and collapsed. The guard shoved past Toby with his club poised. Abel rolled sideways and tried to rise. The club caught him on the right shoulder.

Toby, who had learned a whole profane vocabulary over the past year, swung the guard around calling him every name he knew. The burly guard reacted in two ways: he got red in the face and raised the club. Toby caught it in the middle and, although the burly guard outweighed Toby by fifteen pounds, the difference between them was one of pure strength against weight alone.

They stood eye to eye as Toby slowly forced the club down, tore it from the guard's hands, and punched the guard in the stomach, forcing him back in pain.

Across the corridor 'Pifas yelled. "Kill him! Beat his brains out!"

The commotion brought two other guards. One, younger and faster, appeared in the doorway where he stopped dead still as Toby faced him with the club. The second guard came up, stopped and spoke in a level, quiet tone of voice. "Drop the club, Toby. Drop it! You won't leave here alive if you don't. Use your head. You got less'n a year to go. *Drop it!*"

Behind him Abel spoke unsteadily. "Drop it, Toby. It'll go hard on both of us if you don't."

Toby let the club fall. The burly guard pushed past, looking ashen. As he left the cell, prisoners jeered him.

The young guard picked up the club as the older guard entered the cell. He helped Abel back onto the cot, faced around as solemn as an owl. "You'll get the pit, Toby," he said and left the cell.

The young guard stood outside to close and lock the gate. From out there he said, "Bannion'll make you wish you was dead for hittin' him."

Six guards came for Toby, formed around him for the march to the dingy office of the captain of the guards, a towering man with a bloodless slit of a mouth and eyes as cold as ice. He stood behind a desk, dismissed the guards, stared at Toby a long time before speaking. "What's wrong with you? Strikin' a guard can get another year added to your sentence."

"Abel's sick, Mister," Toby said. "He's been ailin' for a long time, an' he's not eighteen, he's fourteen. He's not strong. Mister Bannion hit him while he was trying to stand up."

The large man's expression did not change. He might as well have been deaf. There were no mitigating circumstances for striking a guard. None at all. He slowly shook his head. "You got a good record. Otherwise I'd keep you here another year. Ten days in the hole. Next time I'll add five years to your time."

The same six guards took Toby behind the mess hall. The pit was a hand-dug hole barely high enough for a man to stand upright and no more than eight feet wide. When the grating was closed — and locked — the only light came through the grating. It was cold but there was something else: Toby was not alone. From holes in the earthen walls water-dogs poked their heads out and barked. The sound more nearly resembled a belch, but they were called water-dogs because to someone it had sounded like a bark.

Water-dogs were some kind of harmless lizard that lived in the ground. It required no more than a day or two of their racket to get on a man's nerves.

Instead of three meals a day Toby was fed twice, once about daybreak when everyone ate, and again at supper time when the cold was returning. Both meals consisted of a bottle of water and gruel so thin he drank it. In the pit, prisoners were not allowed to have eating utensils and everything was removed from their pockets.

On the fourth day the older guard appeared with Toby's supper. After handing down the pails and re-locking the grate, the guard lingered to roll and light a smoke. He was uncomfortable and showed it. The other guards never said a word; this man hunkered over the grating to smoke and finally say, "They're goin' to let you out in the morning."

After that he continued to hunker until he killed his smoke and spoke again. "Abel died this morning."

Toby looked up. The guard was gone.

The pain of loss was acute. It always was, beginning with finding Buttercup shot to death. When morning arrived, only three guards came to help him out of the hole. One of them said gruffly he could eat in the mess hall; it was empty; everyone else had been fed.

He let them take him to the mess hall, but he did not eat even when the cook set fried mush and molasses in front of him.

The guards were mute, like owls. The cook knew only that a man from the pit would be starving. He stood with hands on hips, glaring. "Somethin' wrong with fried grits'n black coffee?"

One of the guards growled for the cook to go back to his kitchen.

They returned Toby to the cell. Abel's bunk had been neatly made. None of his pitiful few possessions was left. Toby's eyes burned so he went to the rear wall with the slit-window overhead, leaned there with both arms folded across his forehead — and cried.

He could not sleep. The following morning that towering captain of the guard came into the cell leaving other guards outside. He handed Toby a slip of paper as he said, "You're released." He held out one hand holding a silver dollar. "Take it!"

Toby faced the larger man. "How did he die?"

"Everyone dies. You was right. He was sick."

"Bannion helped him die."

"Take the dollar. You can ride the prison wagon to the settlement." When Toby still refused to take the dollar, the towering man left the cell, told the guards to leave it open, and walked away.

Toby sat on the edge of the bunk, gazing across at the neatly made bunk. That older guard who had visited him at the hole said, "Leave, Toby. Don't fret. Abel's in a better place."

Stung, Toby turned, facing the guard. "I expect he is. Compared to this place, hell would be like paradise."

The older man was placating but his two younger companions were hostile and wary; they held their clubs in both hands.

As Toby left the cell, a work party was returning from the quarry. 'Pifas was among them. He called to Toby in Spanish. A guard who understood poked him hard in the back as the work party moved along.

Toby remembered the sounds without having the faintest idea what they meant. He declined a ride in the prison wagon. Four guards opened the massive gates. Toby followed the ruts in the direction of that sordid little hamlet, reaching there with the overhead sun giving very little warmth. Early springtime was an unpredictable mixture of tantalizing warmth and bitter cold.

There was a shabby saloon which, fortunately, was operated by a former inmate of the prison. When Toby walked in, he was immediately sized up. The barman put a bottle and small glass atop the bar before Toby reached it and said, "I got no money, Mister."

"You didn't take the dollar, eh? Well, neither did I. Drink up." While Toby was considering the glass, the barman studied him and asked a question. "How old are you, partner?"

"Past eighteen. Why? You don't sell drinks if they're younger?"

"No. I'd sell drinks to a baby. I figured you was maybe a tad older . . . twenty, maybe."

Toby downed the whiskey and had a coughing fit. The barman smiled; he'd pegged Toby for someone unaccustomed to hard liquor. You couldn't operate a bar for long before you could tell the real men from the near-men. The barman refilled the glass. Toby was wiping his eyes when he shook his head and said, "Is there a stage out of here?"

"There's a mud wagon belongs to a feller who's waitin' for his boy to get out. Where do you want to go?"

"South."

"South . . . where?"

"It don't matter, just south until everythin' looks different."

"That'll be a long way, friend. The old man's mud wagon can take you about fifty miles. He don't go no farther south'n Coldstream." The saloonman took a silver dollar from a drawer and slapped it atop the bar. "That ain't charity, Mister. That's for not takin' their damned blood money out yonder. Go ahead, take it. Like I said . . . I do that to everyone of 'em who comes in here after refusin' the prison dollar. An' you better hustle your bustle. Ol' Man Walker's ready to pull out southward directly. Across the road where you see some log corrals. Good luck, partner. One word of advice . . . don't never come back."

Old Man Walker's rig had a light, compact body and wheels shod with extra wide tires, a genuine mud wagon. It was old; the paint was either completely gone or so badly checked the lettering was unreadable. Old Man Walker was the same: faded, old, squinched-up, gray eyes and just enough hair on top to let it grow long on one side so he could sweep it over the bald dome-skin.

He told Toby to ride on top with him. He had no other passengers, but he had some light freight stored inside. If the rig was ancient and so was Mr. Walker, his four-horse hitch consisted of very good animals, well cared for and in their prime. He drove them like they were his children — which they would continue to be for another three years when his son was released.

If Mr. Walker had a first name, Toby never learned it. He chewed and spit often and when he was good and ready he started talking. "My boy got six years half over with now . . . for shootin' a son-of-a-bitch that needed killin' ten times over. What'd you say your name was?"

Toby hadn't said. "Toby Lincoln."

"Fine name, Mister Lincoln."

Toby had a flash of memory about someone he had known who wouldn't have agreed with that and wore the buttons to prove it.

"I was in Mister Lincoln's Army. We had to chase them Rebels all over the South before we cornered 'em close by the Appomattox court house. You know, when they give up an' I went amongst 'em, it was a sight a man'd never forget. Mostly they had no shoes. They had cracked corn in one pocket, musket balls'n molasses-cured chewin' tobacco in the other pocket."

The old man sat hunched in silence for a long time before speaking again. "My boy'll be thirty-five when he gets free. You'll be younger'n that I'd guess."

"A few years younger, Mister Walker. I'm crowdin' twenty." Toby was expecting questions he did not want to answer, so he changed the subject. "Have you ever been in New Mexico, Mister Walker?"

The old man spat, cleared his throat, and looked around at Toby. "Ever been there? I was born down there; so was my boy. Do you expect to go there?"

"I just want to leave this country far behind."

The old man sat straighter on the seat, expectorated again, then said, "Well now. What part of New Mexico?"

"I don't know. I never been there."

"I see. I been all over New Mexico territory. Was raised talkin' Mex as much as English. You want some advice?"

"I'll listen, Mister Walker."

"Where I leave you off down at Coldstream, from there you can ride a Cartwright stage down to the New Mexico line. When you get over the line, travel southeast to a place called Trabajo. I got no idea why it has that name. It means work in Spanish. They don't do no more work in Trabajo than they can help doin'. When you get there, look up a ranch called Trinitaria. Tell them Dale Walker sent you. They'll give you work." The old man sprayed amber again before continuing. "Trinitaria belonged to my cousin's husband. He was a Mexican. I left down there when my boy got into trouble. I'll come back when he gets out. You tell 'em I said that. Can you speak Mex?"

Toby shook his head. "I have a hard enough time with English."

"Well, they'll teach you. You ever done any range work?"

"Some."

The old man interpreted that correctly. "They'll teach you. Mostly they got *vaqueros* . . . Mexican cowboys. What'd you say your name was?"

"Toby Lincoln."

The old man nodded. "I forget names. I didn't mean no slight."

Toby lightly slapped the old man on the shoulder. "Trinitaria?"

"Yep. Trinitaria. It's a big ranch. Mostly from an old Spanish grant. If the land was better, the gringos would have taken it, but all that's past now."

"What does Trinitaria mean?"

"Somethin' like a place to rest, a place where a man can settle in an' as they say in Spanish . . . be tranquil."

When they reached the village of Coldstream, the old stager climbed stiffly down to unload his freight. Toby helped; the old man managed to avoid the heaviest crates which Toby handled as though they were weightless. When the mud wagon was empty, the stager stood in shade wiping sweat while Toby considered the village. It had acquired its name from someone with more hope than common sense. There was a creek for water, but it had crossed many miles of open country before reaching the village. The result was that the person who had named the place after the creek must not have tested the water; it was not cold; it was lukewarm and muddy.

The old stager studied Toby, fished in a pocket, produced a silver cartwheel, and held it out. Toby looked down and shook his head. The ride to this place had cost him two-bits so he still had seventy-five cents.

The old man said, "Take it, boy. I got six more an' you're goin' to need it. Take it!"

Toby took the money and would have expressed his gratitude but old Walker was already climbing back to the high seat to gather his lines and turn back. He looked down just once. "Remember . . . Trinitaria."

The coach made a wide sashay before straightening up to head back the way it had come.

There was a Cartwright coach leaving Coldstream for the south country on which Toby bought passage as far as Trabajo. It was a measure of his tiredness that he slept all the way. He was awakened by a rough shake, climbed out of the coach, looked around, and decided Trabajo was an ugly place of mud buildings and what seemed to be irresponsible squalor. He went to the trading barn where a black man was finishing his chores. When Toby asked about renting a horse, the black man asked why. Toby told him about Trinitaria, his destination.

The black man led the way to a huge, old, unkempt tree and while standing in its shade he raised an arm. "There's a road. See it out yonder?"

Toby saw it. It was not exactly a road; it was two wide wagon ruts leading eastward and somewhat southward. He nodded as the black man lowered his arm. "Six, eight miles. Follow the road an' you'll fetch up in the yard. If you keep the horse until tomorrow . . . two bits."

Toby counted out the coins which the black man also counted before leading the way to a ramshackle shed in which he lived, and which was also where he kept his saddles and harness. He rigged out a big roman-nosed bay horse with little pig-eyes, handed Toby the reins, and said, "Stay on the road. If you don't bring the horse back tomorrow, I'll have to charge you another two bits."

Toby left the village on the meandering wagon road with the black man watching him from beneath the shade tree. If others also saw him depart from Trabajo, he knew nothing about it. He did not look back, not even once.

He was riding a powerful, big, ugly, bay horse with hope in his heart. If they didn't hire him on at Trinitaria, he'd still have more than a dollar to keep him going until he got hired on somewhere else.

Since leaving the north country he had noticed subtle — and sometimes not so subtle — changes. For one thing there were more dark-looking people than he'd ever seen before. Another thing was the lack of big trees, pines and firs, fewer watercourses, and the heat was different. A man sweated in New Mexico territory while up north, springtime or not, it paid to keep a coat handy.

He saw cattle. Up north, stockmen had been upgrading livestock for several decades because short-legged, full-bodied, white-faced critters put on better weight and brought more money than slab-sided, wicked-horned, long-legged critters who would fight a buzz-saw.

New Mexico had yet to make the transition. The livestock Toby saw did not give an inch as he rode past them. Mostly, they were slick but not fat. They were also mottled and had spreads of horns he guessed to be maybe six feet from tip to tip. Before he saw buildings in the distance, he decided these New Mexico cattle would be hard to handle and, with the sun reddening over his shoulder to the west, he saw the scattering of buildings up ahead with pole corrals built to a height of about six feet. He thought that those animals he had seen could probably jump a fence built higher than a horse could jump.

He studied the buildings. Mostly, they had low roofs, the kind that up north would collapse under the weight of snow the first winter, but they were clearly old structures which was heartening.

If Toby never saw four-foot snow drifts the rest of his life, he would be everlastingly thankful.

Chapter Seven

Trinitaria

It helped that Toby had minimal experience, and knowledge, of cattle outfits because in the south desert country the large ranches did not hire seasonal riders as was done up north. South desert outfits had resident riders, some second and third generation *vaqueros* who lived in the *jacales* around the yard. Their women did the cooking and raised the children.

When Toby tied up out front of the massive adobe barn a dark, older man with skin the shade and texture of old leather came out. His hair was white, making quite a contrast to the darkness of his skin. He had a fierce dragoon mustache, also white, and, although he smiled as he came to the tie-rack, his tawny-tan eyes were wary and assessing.

Toby mentioned the stager named Walker. The Mexican showed no expression but politely inclined his head. When Toby asked about getting hired on, the Mexican looked him up and down, looked at the pig-eyed ugly horse and said, "You don't have no outfit?"

Toby felt uncomfortable under the shrewd, knowing eyes of the older man. "No sir. I had one once, couple years back, but lost it."

"Where are you from?" the older man asked.

"Well, from a railroad siding town, and later I worked

for Mister Roberts on his ranch in Colorado."

The Mexican was clearly having doubts. He leaned on the tie rack gazing in the direction of the *patrón*'s large, massive adobe house which was almost completely surrounded by a six-foot mud wall.

Toby guessed the Mexican was indecisive for other reasons and said, "Mister, I work hard. Never worked any other way. What I don't know I'll pick up fast."

The Mexican returned his gaze to Toby. He almost smiled. No man lived to be sixty without understanding desperation when he saw — or heard — it. He said, "Wait here," and walked in the direction of the low, rambling house. He passed through an old wooden gate and disappeared.

A dark woman as shapeless as a barrel and just as round came along, smiled at Toby and said, *"Buenos dias, vaquero."*

It was her dazzling smile that told him whatever she had said was meant to be pleasant. He removed his old hat and slightly bowed as he smiled back.

The hefty woman had a complexion of peaches and cream. She went as far as a nearby *jacal,* poked her head in, said something in rapid Spanish, and walked on.

Moments later two women and a man emerged from the *jacal* to stare. One of the women was wrinkled as a prune; the other woman was much younger. The man was spare, sinewy, of medium height with eyes as black as obsidian. He stared — they all did — without speaking or nodding.

Toby wearied of waiting and led his horse in search of water. The trough was behind the barn where an extensive series of working corrals made of lodgepole pines had striped shade. He waited until the horse had finished and leaned down also to drink.

While he was doing this, the white-headed Mexican came around back and said, "What is your name?"

"Toby Lincoln. What's yours?"

"Leon Salázar. I am the *mayordomo* of. . . ."

"By any chance are you kin to a feller I knew named Epifanio Salazar?"

For five seconds the *mayordomo* squinted at Toby before giving his head a tight little negative shake. "I started to say I am the *mayordomo* of Rancho Trinitaria. *La patrona* said to hire you if we need another rider."

Toby beamed. "I'm obliged."

Salazar rolled his shoulders in a small gesture. "I will saddle a horse for you so that you can return the black man's horse and have something to ride back on."

Toby watched everything the *mayordomo* did, took the reins and would have swung up, but the *mayordomo* said, "No! Never get on a horse inside a building." He turned his back, rolled his eyes, and led the way out into the heat-rising morning. "Now get on," he said. "I'll bring the other horse."

As Toby left the yard, people came silently to stand near the *mayordomo* and watched. Once, a rider said something in Spanish which earned him murmurs of approval, but not from the *mayordomo*, "He is young."

"And very strong," the barrel-shaped woman said.

The *mayordomo* ignored that. "*La patrona* knows someone he knows, so we hire him." The *mayordomo* did not look pleased, nor was he. He had lived at Trinitaria since childhood. He had served *el viejo,* the old *patrón,* as a young man; his father, as a middle-aged man, had become *mayordomo* shortly before the old man had died; and now he served the only surviving member of the family, the last *patrón*'s widowed granddaughter, Lillian Monteverde. He spoke good English but was more comfortable in Spanish. He was also more familiar with the idiosyncrasies of his own people than he was with *gringos.*

When a man passes sixty, he is more apt to shrug at the perversities of God than he is at twenty. Salazar stood watching the diminishing figure of the *gringo* riding a Trinitaria horse and leading the other horse. 'Pifas Salazar, that *muy matador,* was the only son of the *mayordomo* so, if this Toby Lincoln had known 'Pifas, it had to be in prison.

When Toby reached the village and handed over the ugly bay horse, the black horse trader saw the Trinitaria brand on the left shoulder of the horse Toby had arrived on. He took the rope to his horse and said, "They hired you?"

Toby swung to the ground. "You sound surprised. They hired me."

The black man was considering the returned animal when he said, "My guess is that you ain't no *vaquero.* I am surprised. Old Salazar don't like *gringos* an' they don't need riders. They raise their own."

Toby considered the black man. "All their riders live on the ranch?"

"Yes. Family after family of 'em. Leon Salazar's paw worked for Trinitaria. Leon's top dog." He pronounced it lay-own, not lee-on.

"What kind of feller is he?"

The black man answered forthrightly. "Don't never lie to him. Do what you're told. He's a good man in his own way." The horse trader put a quizzical gaze on Toby. "If you last a month, I'll be surprised. Them folks out there is real stockraisers. Top-notch riders, ropers, an' they'll expect you to be as good. Well, as good as you can be anyway. You owe me another two bits."

Toby handed over the coins, led his Trinitaria horse

to a stone trough to drink, and the black man yelled at him. "Take the bridle off. A horse drinkin' aroun' the bit sucks air. If he gets a bellyache on you, you'll end up leadin' him."

Toby removed the bridle. He stood in shade until the horse was tanked up, then re-bridled him and was about to mount and ride up through the barn runway, when he remembered. He led the horse all the way to the roadway where scrawny chickens pecked and several old men dozed on a bench outside the *cantina,* mounted, and started back following the same meandering ruts he had used before.

The matter of wages had not been mentioned by the *mayordomo.* Toby did not care. What did bother him was where he would eat and sleep. Up north cattle outfits had cook shacks and bunkhouses. Down here it seemed every rider had his own little adobe house and a woman to feed him.

The heat came, which it would continue to do now until winter. Springtime was very brief. Autumn was even more so. Even when winter set in although a rider needed a coat, for a couple of months, he needed a poncho more. When it rained, water came down like a fat cow peeing on a flat rock.

Once he reached the shaded yard, there was not a soul in sight and the corralled using-stock stood hip-shot in shade occasionally switching their tails as they dozed. It was afternoon and it was hot.

He led the Trinitaria horse into the cool, shadowy barn to off-saddle him, heard a faint sound, and turned. It was an old woman, lined and wizened, with bright black eyes. She smiled and spoke in fair English. "I know you. You are my man before he rode away an' never come back. Sixteen years ago. You look like him but you should be much older."

Toby stood in motionless silence.

The old woman came out of the shadows. She was unkempt with straggling hair as gray as dawn. Her face was a washboard of wrinkles. Her snake-bright eyes were fixed on Toby as she said, "How can you be so young? You didn't look this young sixteen years ago. How did you do it? Did you come because Enrique died? He had your eyes and chin. Someone told you the snake bite killed him?"

Toby slowly went back to off-saddling. The old woman made him uncomfortable. He slung the rig over a saddle pole, led the horse out back inside the corral before removing the bridle. When he started back to the barn, the old woman was in the doorway. "Why won't you talk to me? How did you know about Enrique?"

Toby went past, draped the bridle over the saddle horn, kept his back to the old woman and would have left the barn but she got in front of him no more than fifteen feet away and spoke again.

"Come home. I will fix *fajitas* the way you liked them. Come along. I have two pictures of Enrique."

When Toby did not move, the old woman plucked at his sleeve. *"Come,"* she said, this time in Spanish, and smiled up into his face. *"Come, mi amor,"* and switched back to English to also say, "I know, I never forgot. You don't like me to talk in Mexican. I won't do it again. Now come."

Her tugging was insistent. Toby hung back but the old woman raised her voice so he allowed her to take him as far as the front barn opening.

Up there a woman with a stunning appearance stood like a statue. She had pigeon-wings of pale silver at each temple. She was tall and spare. Her mouth was wide and full-lipped. She ignored Toby and spoke quietly in Spanish to the old woman who did not release her grip on Toby's sleeve. The handsome woman came slowly toward them, shot Toby a peculiar look, half embarrassed, half annoyed, freed the old woman's fingers, took her hand in a soft grip and finally acknowledged Toby's presence. Half in English.

"She is really my *cuñada* . . . but I've always called her *Tía* Maria."

Toby nodded about that without speaking.

The handsome woman hesitated. Toby guessed her problem; the old woman spoke both English and Spanish which made it impossible for the stunning woman to offer any more of an explanation, but she said, "You are the man the *mayordomo* hired today?"

"Yes'm. Toby Lincoln, ma'am."

The old woman was now tugging at the handsome woman, who resisted her long enough to say, "I want to talk to you. Later. Come to the house after sundown."

Toby watched the handsome woman being pulled toward the massive, low and long residence of *la patrona* of Trinitaria.

He went back deeper into the barn as Leon Salazar came in from out back. The *mayordomo* paused to scratch vigorously inside his shirt as he gazed at Toby. "I thought I heard voices," he said.

"I was off-saddling when a real old woman . . . I didn't hear her until she was close by. . . ."

Salazar nodded. "*Tía* Maria."

"I guess so. Mister Salazar, is there something wrong with her?"

The *mayordomo* looked for something to sit on, found a rickety three-legged stool, sat down, and said, "*Tía* Maria is. . . ."

"What does *tía* mean?"

"Aunt. Aunt Maria is the sister of the dead *patrón*. The *patrón* hired a *gringo* cowboy. A Texan named Ruben. Maria fell in love with him. The *patrón* said he would fire Ruben. He was mad. His sister said she would kill herself. The *patrón* gave them a *jacal* on the ranch. Maria had a child . . . Enrique." Salazar paused. "A good boy, handsome too. Maria loved him very much.

"One day in springtime when we all went out to bring in the horses, in all the dust and noise no one noticed until we were at the corrals . . . Ruben was not there."

"How long ago, Mister Salazar?"

"I'm not sure. Sixteen, eighteen years ago. He never came back. The women cared for Maria and after some years she learned to smile again. Until Enrique went out with us two years ago to hunt bulls. A rattlesnake bit him in the side. He died. Maria did not recover that time." Salazar arose, looking out of the barn across the sweltering yard toward the main house. "They keep her over there. There have been doctors come and go." Salazar shrugged. "What did she say to you?"

"She thought I was her husband come back."

"They were never married; *el patrón* would not permit it. You do look a little like Ruben. Not very much, but a little."

Salazar gazed at Toby. "Did someone come for her?"

"Yes. A tall woman with gray at the temples. She said the old woman was her aunt."

Salazar inclined his head. "That was *la patrona, Dona* Lillian." Salazar ruefully smiled. "Her mother was a *gringa* from the East somewhere. She died when the daughter was eleven years old. She is buried at the graveyard behind the house."

Salazar changed the subject. "You eat with me tonight.

My wife died seven years ago, but I have a friend who can cook better than anyone. Tomorrow we will get you settled. Now, come to supper with me." As he was turning to lead the way, Salazar said, "Did you visit the *cantina* in town?"

"No. I don't much care for the taste of whiskey."

Salazar smiled. "Then never try pulque or tequila," he said.

The *mayordomo*'s cook was the woman with the barrel shape who smiled broadly at Toby, said something in Spanish to the *mayordomo,* who looked Toby up and down and agreed that he looked like a tramp. She told Salazar to make him respectable and the *mayordomo* inclined his head.

Toby bedded down in a musty-smelling old *jacal.* He was tired but did not sleep for a long time. Too many things were different, including supper. It was good but different. And there was the language. It sounded like a combination of trilling music and croaking frogs. And — the old woman, Aunt — no *tía,* he had to learn the language, *Tía* Maria, it hurt his heart to think back to their meeting. She was old, wrinkled, *loco en la cabeza* — crazy in the head — but so pathetic, so. . . . He sat straight up; he had forgotten he was supposed to go to the main house tonight — last night then. The stunning woman might have him fired. She had left Toby with the impression she would not forgive an oversight.

He said, "Hell!" and went to sleep.

In the morning there were cooking fires with fragrant smoke coming from among the little houses of the retainers. Old Salazar met him at the corrals, told him to come and eat the day's first meal with him. This time the barrel-shaped woman eyed him askance and barely smiled. She spoke in Spanish to the *mayordomo* who nodded and addressed Toby. "*La patrona* was here. You were supposed to go to the main house last night."

Toby said, "I forgot."

The *mayordomo* and his friend gazed solemnly at Toby before Salazar spoke. "Friend, you do not forget when *la patrona* tells you to do something. Never."

Toby had a feeling of guilt and showed it. "Should I go over there an' apologize?"

Salazar emptied a coffee cup before replying. "No. She went to Trabajo this morning. When she comes back, I'll ask if she still wants to see you."

The woman spoke in Spanish. "*Jefe,* he is young."

Salazar looked around to answer her in the same language. "There is no excuse and you know it."

The woman rolled her eyes. "He is new. Give him time."

This time Salazar turned completely to face the cook. He was slow to speak but eventually he said, "He is too young for you. I'll speak for him."

The woman said no more. She had already said more than she should have. Like *la patrona,* the *mayordomo*'s word was law.

Toby rode out with the *vaqueros,* one of whom was a thin man called Desdentado because he had no teeth. He was as old as Salazar, maybe older (no one knew for certain, not even Desdentado). He spoke very good English despite an inability to pronounce letters his lack of teeth made difficult.

He was sprightly, laughed, and was one of the best stockmen on Trinitaria. The other riders varied in age from roughly Toby's age to much older. He was to learn with men of oily dark skin it was difficult accurately to guess ages.

They did not laugh at Toby's mistakes and general ignorance, but they smiled and winked at each other from time to time.

The first day out because the others called Salazar *jefe,* Toby also did — without the faintest notion whether it was a name or another of those designations like the one they used for Manual Acosta — Desdentado.

They returned to the yard with the sun slanting away, with shadows forming and with a wizened old man the color of ancient leather standing in the barn doorway. As soon as they dismounted, the old man spoke sharply to Salazar in Spanish. The *mayordomo* turned toward Toby. "*La patrona* wants you at the house."

Toby nodded, led his animal inside to be off-saddled, and met Salazar's hostile glare. Toby finished with the horse, said he'd wash out back at the trough, then go across the yard.

Salazar exploded. "I told you . . . when she says for someone to come . . . it means right now. *¡Andale!* Go! Wash later. *¡Pronto!*"

Toby crossed the yard stinging from the *mayordomo*'s anger, and also with misgivings about what lay ahead. One thing seemed to be an immutable fact in this country: when someone with authority told a man to do something, it meant right now.

He opened the heavy old wooden gate, entered the patio where shade was everywhere, approached the massive oaken door with its hand-wrought bolt heads, and knocked. Nothing happened until a squatty Indian woman opened the door, frowning. She pointed to an old bell half hidden by a flowering bush. She also pointed to an old wooden bench and told him to sit down — in Spanish. He nodded as she closed the door, sat on the bench, impressed with the variety of flowering plants, unaware how threadbare he looked because he had never looked otherwise.

The beautiful tall woman came out, looked at Toby wearing a faint frown. Then she shrugged. He was obviously hopelessly ignorant. Even in the States seated men arose when a woman appeared.

She did not sit; she stood backgrounded by some bush with large, blood-red flowers. As long as Toby lived, when he thought of her, this was how he remembered the woman.

She had only the barest accent when she used English. Something else he would learn about Lillian Monteverde — she was direct.

Her first words were: "The *jefe* told you about my aunt?"

Toby nodded. "Yes. Ma'am, what does *jefe* mean?"

She relaxed slightly, went to a bench, sat down, and inwardly sighed. Strong as an ox and twice as dense. "It means 'chief.' Salazar is what *gringos* call a foreman; the man in charge who is responsible only to me."

He reddened for no particular reason and smiled. "Thank you. I never heard that much Spanish before."

She let that pass. "Tell me about yourself, Toby Lincoln."

"There isn't much to tell, ma'am."

"Your parents . . . ?"

"My father died. My mother had other kids. She left me at a home."

"Do you remember her?"

"Yes. I was about ten when she left me there."

The handsome woman considered Toby. It was obvious this conversation pained him, so she said, "Why were you in prison?"

The surprise was total. He sat gazing at her in long silence. "Why? Because they said I stole a horse."

"Did you?"

"No ma'am. I worked for a man named Roberts. He gave me the horse when he fired me."

"Why did he fire you?"

Chapter Eight

From Trinitaria to Trabajo

Her questions did not bother him, very much anyway, but how she had known he had been in prison *did* bother him. It was a while before she allowed him an opportunity to ask his own questions.

Her voice was neither hard nor soft. Her words were brusque and direct. When she asked him how long he had been in New Mexico and why he was here, he told her the truth. "I got some poor memories of up north an'. . . ."

"And you wanted to leave them behind. How old are you?"

"Goin' onto twenty-one."

She leaned with hands clasped between her knees. "They will travel with you . . . always. I'm older than you. You can't forget them nor run away from them. That's what life is made of: memories."

"Yes'm."

"But you can train yourself not to think of unpleasant ones."

"Yes'm. Is it all right if I ask a question?"

She nodded.

"How did you know I'd been in prison?"

She pulled down a deep breath looking steadily at him. There was so much he did not know. She spoke quietly at some length. "In this country most things are different from where you've been."

He nodded about that; they were for a fact.

"*Jefe* Salazar's son is Epifanio Salazar. You asked him yesterday if he knew anyone by that name. He did not explain it to you but when he came to the main house he told me you had been in prison with his son."

Toby relaxed on the bench. He'd been in awe of her, had thought she was going to fire him. He also thought she was the most beautiful female-woman he had ever seen.

She almost smiled at him. "You need new clothes."

He reddened. "Yes'm. Come payday I'll go to that village back yonder. If they have clothes there. . . ."

"They have. The store is opposite the *cantina*." She arose. "My aunt. . . ."

He interrupted her. "Your *tía*."

Just for a moment her eyes hardened toward him. Interrupting a speaker was bad manners everywhere, not just in New Mexico. Then she smiled. "*Tía* is right. I think you will pick up the language. My *tía* thinks you are the husband who deserted her many years ago."

He also stood up. "Yes'm. I sure wasn't expectin' anyone like her when I come back from Trabajo. I didn't know what to say."

She continued as though he had not spoken. "I keep her in the house. There is a woman who takes care of her. Sometimes she comes out here and sits in the shade, and sleeps. Yesterday she saw you coming back from the village. You do resemble her Texan a little. From a distance. . . ." The beautiful woman shrugged. "She told me last night she must have a new dress. She wanted to show you a photograph of her son, who died two years ago."

"Mister Salazar told me . . . rattler got him."

As before she continued as though he had not spoken. "She wants to go to her old little house and cook for you." The woman's eyes wavered. "I have known her all my life. She was my husband's sister. He was older than I. Maria was like a mother. This is the first time she did this . . . saw someone she thinks is her Texan returning. She was difficult. She wanted to go make supper for you in the little house last night."

Toby sank back down on the bench. It did not require any degree of brilliance to understand where this conversation was going. He said, "I'll leave." He stood up. "I'm sorry, ma'am."

Lillian Monteverde crossed over, lightly laying a hand on his arm as she softly said, "I'm sorry too," and went into the house.

As he crossed toward the barn, he looked around. Unconsciously he had begun to appreciate this big ranch with its permanent retainers, the way they lived, all together in their little mud houses — with laughter, noisy children, sometimes music in the evenings, words to the music he did not understand — the sense of comradeship, of belonging, which he had never known and now felt he might have become a part of. It was what he wanted most out of life.

The *mayordomo* was waiting, smoking a little brown-paper *cigarillo* and making it appear he just happened to be standing there when Toby came up. *Mayordomo* Salazar had watched him crossing from the house. When a man has seen much of life, he can sense things. Salazar ground his cigarette underfoot as he said, "Well, *compañero* . . . ?"

Toby had no idea men used that term with other men only when they were fond of them. Right then, if he had known, it would not have made any difference. "I need to borrow a horse. I'll leave him with the horse trader in Trabajo."

Salazar nodded without asking the obvious question, jerked his head, and led off toward his *jacal.* The barrel-shaped woman with the beautiful complexion was not there. They sat at the hand-made, rough table. Salazar brought a bottle and two tin cups. He barely tipped a faintly opaque liquid into one cup, more into his own cup, put the bottle aside, and raised his cup. In Spanish he said, "May God be with you. Somewhere may your life become tranquil."

Toby smiled. It might as well have been Greek but he raised the cup, drained it, and water rushed into his eyes. Salazar affected not to notice. "I want to tell you something. That man you asked me about . . . Epifanio . . . he is my son. He will maybe die in prison for his crime. The only way you could have known him was in prison."

Toby nodded while wiping his eyes with a sleeve. He already knew this. But what Salazar said next made Toby forget to wipe his eyes. "In a letter from him someone got out of the prison he told me about a boy called Abel. How a guard called Bannion beat him with a club and he died."

Toby unconsciously pushed the tin cup aside. The pain of recollection made it momentarily difficult to speak. He stared at the older man without seeing the *mayordomo*'s face; in its place was Abel's expression of agony after he had been struck.

Salazar's gaze did not waver nor blink. "This man Bannion in my son's letter is coming to Trabajo with a prison wagon for two men who stole cattle and sold them down in Mexico. Trinitaria cattle." Salazar paused to tip more liquor into his cup and drink it. He made no offer of liquor to Toby as he leaned back off the table. "Do you want the man Bannion?" he asked.

Toby nodded and would have spoken but Salazar held up a hand. "Wait. Now listen to me. Do you know how to use a gun?"

"I never shot one, if that's what you mean."

"Toby, guards on prison wagons know how to use guns. Some of them are very good." Salazar shrugged. "It don't matter at the prison whether they bring back prisoners dead or alive. Do you understand what I am saying? If you want this man, you have to know how to protect yourself." Salazar leaned on the table. "You know Desdentado?"

"Manual Acosta? Yes, I know him."

"Let me tell you . . . he is good-natured, laughs and smiles. In Mexico he is wanted for killing seven men. Soldiers he fought as a *pronunciado*. He killed each of them in a fair fight. There is no more deadly man anywhere than Desdentado. For your own sake let's go talk to him."

Toby frowned. "I don't need Acosta to settle. . . ."

Salazar exploded. "*¡Estupido gringo!* He is not going to do the fighting for you! He can teach you how to use a gun. Come along."

When they were outside, Toby stopped. "*Jefe,* how did Epifanio know I was here?"

"He didn't know. He told me the name of the man they released who had been the *compañero* of the one called Abel. He said someday he will kill Bannion himself. Come along."

Desdentado was braiding a pair of rawhide reins when his visitors walked in. His little adobe room was unkempt and sour-smelling. He put the rawhide strips aside, went to a stone oven built into a corner of his house to shake a blackened coffeepot. Salazar shook his head, stood near the table where the lean, wiry man had been working and spoke rapidly in Spanish.

For five seconds affable Manuel Acosta stared at the *mayordomo.* Then he said, "Wait," and left the room. Salazar smiled slightly at Toby. When Acosta returned, he gently placed an obviously well-cared for six-gun on the table. Across the back-strap of the handle were nine diagonal filings.

Desdentado was not smiling. He told Toby to pick up the gun, which was done. Now the toothless man said. "Raise the arm . . . no, bend your elbow. Fine. Now bring the arm down with the gun pointing at me, fast."

Toby obeyed. Desdentado made him repeat the performance three times. After the last time he broke into a wide smile. To Salazar he spoke Spanish. "Good. Very good, *compañero.* Now tell me why you want him to be *muy matador?*"

Salazar repeated the story about Abel, and how he knew this Bannion was coming south. The last thing he said was that some men are born with a debt, some men acquire a debt through life, but whatever the case, it is God's will that a man leave this life debt-free.

Manuel Acosta gazed at the *mayordomo* as he asked a question. "How did 'Pifas know Toby was here?"

"He didn't know it, Manuel. Now do you understand?"

"No."

"Why would 'Pifas write me a letter about this child being killed, naming the man who was responsible? Why would he write Toby's name in a letter to me . . . those names mean nothing to me . . . now do you understand?"

Acosta sat a long time staring at the *mayordomo* before speaking. "*Jefe.* This is God's will for Toby?"

"Yes. This is God's will."

Acosta let go a long breath. "How much time, *jefe?* I can't do it overnight."

The letter had not said when the prison wagon would arrive in Trabajo so Salazar shrugged. "If the wagon left the prison yesterday or today. . . ."

Desdentado looked sly when he said, "I will take him out of earshot and you will make excuses for me not being in the saddle. Is that all right?"

"Except for one thing, Manuel. He is leaving Trinitaria."

"You fired him?"

"No. Someday I shall explain. It's the old aunt." Salazar arose and patted Toby lightly on the shoulder. "You and Manuel work it out. I'll leave a saddled horse in the barn for you to ride to Trabajo."

After Salazar departed, Manuel Acosta sank down again at the table. He seemed unaware of the man across from him for a few moments. He finally said, "You are fired?"

"Yes. Well, it was my idea."

"Because of Aunt Maria?"

"Yes."

Acosta threw up his arms. "Someday *el jefe* will tell me. You are going to stay in Trabajo?"

"Yes."

"Where, then."

"I got no idea. There don't seem to be a boarding house."

Acosta rolled his eyes. "A boarding house? Friend, Trabajo is a place where people sit and wait. There is the *cantina,* the store, the barn of horses and the jail where they keep drunks overnight, and sometimes men like the prison wagon is coming for. But I have a nephew. Look for a man named Ortiz, Sanchez Ortiz. Tell him you need a place to stay, that I sent you, that when I can I will explain. Now then, I will come to Trabajo in the morning. We will ride out and I will show you about the gun."

Toby offered his hand as he stood up. Acosta broadly smiled, shook, and said, *"Por nada."*

The *mayordomo* was waiting in the barn, smoking one of his little brown-paper cigarettes. He looked pensive as Toby walked in out of the heat and stillness. The saddled Trinitaria horse was half asleep with the cinch loose. As Toby came in, Salazar flipped up the stirrup leather and snugged up the cinch. He said, "*La patrona* was here. She wanted to know if you had left. I told her the saddled horse was for you. That you would leave soon. She went back to the house."

Salazar let the stirrup leather fall and looked across the saddle seat at Toby. "She said to give you this." Salazar held out a palm with two silver dollars on it.

Money was something that never had and never would influence Toby very much. He already had two silver dollars in his pocket. He untied the horse to lead it outside before mounting. Salazar followed and when Toby was astride Salazar held up the money again. "Buy some decent clothes and a pair of boots. You earned it. Take it."

Toby took the coins, pocketed them, and held out his hand. "*Jefe,* how long does a man wander before he finds the place he needs?"

Salazar gave Toby's hand an extra hard squeeze and released it before answering. "For you, I don't know. For me, the others like me, it is Trinitaria. Listen to Manuel. If you fight this Bannion, be careful; they come on those wagons in pairs." Salazar pulled his hatbrim low. *"Adios, compañero."*

* * * * *

It was a genuine south desert country scorcher, the kind that even drove descendants of natives to cover and made a man sweat standing still in shade. Because horses had much more exposed hide, they sweated more. By the time Toby reached Trabajo even the vagrant chickens were gone; the single dusty roadway was empty; the bench where old men gathered hadn't had a soul on it since yesterday and the man in the *cantina* had fallen asleep over an ancient newspaper at one of the card tables. He awakened when one of his spindle doors protested years of neglect from an oil can.

He rubbed his eyes on the way behind the bar and did not really look at his only customer until he was back there facing forward. He came alive with a genial smile.

"Sarsaparilla?" he said, and found a bottle which he opened and emptied into a glass for Toby. "Five cents," he said.

Toby placed the nickel atop the bar and leaned without touching the glass. "Hot," he said, and wiped his forehead.

The barman ran a hand over his beard-stubbled face and agreed. "Wait, friend. Another three four weeks an' you can fry eggs on the rocks."

"Do you know a man named Sanchez Ortiz?"

"Everybody knows Sanchez."

"Where does he live?"

"Go around behind the saloon. There's five or six of them Mex adobe shacks . . . they call 'em *jacales* or *chozas*. The one with the old wagon canvas stretched over the front."

"What does he do for a living?"

The barman cocked his head slightly. "Friend, this is Trabajo. There's only one person here I know what he does for a livin'. That's me. I don't know about the others an' don't want to know . . . and don't ask questions."

Toby sipped his sarsaparilla. It was tepid but so was everything else folks drank in the Trabajo country. This time of year it did not have to be cold, just wet.

Toby said his name and the barman nodded. "Yes, I know. In this town a stranger perks up interest."

"Is there a town marshal?"

The barman looked surprised. "There's a constable. Me. You want somebody locked up?"

"This is pretty good sarsaparilla."

"There ain't much demand for sarsaparilla. Used to be a preacher hung around. That's all he drank, sarsaparilla'n water. You got some trouble with the law?"

"No. I was just curious. Seems like there's an awful lot of open country. You ever have stages stopped?"

The barman considered Toby with less amiability. "No, sir, not that I know of an' I been here quite a spell. Stages don't come down this far very often an' when they do all they carry is a passenger now'n then and light freight for the store and what-not."

The barman leaned back off his counter. "Anyone figurin' on stoppin' a stage down here, Mister, would get the disappointment of his life. I ain't even seen a gun-guard on a stage down here since I come to Trabajo. Just the driver is all."

"I heard you got a couple of prisoners locked up over at the jailhouse. How does anyone get 'em away from here without gun-guards?"

The barman rolled his eyes. "Mister, they don't go north from here on stages. There's a special wagon comes for them an' it carries a driver, a guard, and enough guns to fight a small war."

"This wagon's comin' for your prisoners? What did they do?"

"Stole cattle, run 'em down over the line an' sold 'em in Mexico. I guess they been doin' it for a long time, but they only stole a few head at a time. They was *coyote* to do it that way . . . but the smartest rustler on earth'll get caught sometime."

"An' the wagon'll come an' take them to prison?"

"Yep. It ain't had to come here for several years. The last time some damned drunk shot a Mex *arriero* in the back. When that bullet hit him, you could hear them little bells they wear on the side of their pants tinkle all the way down to the trader's barn."

"They hauled him away in the wagon?"

"Yep. But the wagon didn't get down here for damned near a week an' the town had to feed him. Just before the wagon come, some of the fellers around town come in here for whiskey, talkin' of hangin' the son-of-a-bitch. I talked 'em out of it, an' as luck would have it the wagon arrived the next day."

"How about the prisoners you got now?"

"Well, the circuit ridin' judge was here two weeks ago. He sentenced 'em, an' he always writes the prison where they are an' all. I'd guess, goin' on what I know, the wagon'll be along for them two maybe within the next four or five days. I hope so. Folks don't like to have to pay for feedin' prisoners."

Toby finished his sarsaparilla, thanked the barman, and went in search of the Ortiz adobe.

The barman stared at his swinging doors long after Toby had departed. If that damned fool figured to stop a stage in this country, he had to be either awful hard up or crazy. For what he might get, coins from the driver and maybe a bottle or two of whiskey, the risk wasn't worth it. As far as the barman knew, no highwayman had ever been shot stopping a coach in the Trabajo country, but there could always be a first time.

The barman got himself a jolt and lingered over it. Trabajo would sure as hell get yanked wide awake if someone did rob a stage.

The barman finished his whiskey and smiled to himself. There'd be lawmen swarming over the countryside. What had made him smile was a notion he had entertained for a long time that among the folks living in and around Trabajo were wanted men from up north resting on their way to the border. If they made it over the line down into Mexico, U.S. law couldn't touch them.

If lawmen came down here now, at the height of the southward exodus of wanted fugitives, for the folks around Trabajo it would be like shaking a blanket to rid it of ants; horsemen would be scattering every which way, mostly southward.

Chapter Nine

At Trinitaria a Crisis

The residence of Sanchez Ortiz was indeed distinguishable by the old wagon-bow canvas which shaded the front of the house as well as a small front area with two old chairs. That canvas was called a "texas" by the Mexicans and for a fact it made the front and the interior many degrees cooler.

Sanchez Ortiz surprised Toby; he did not seem any older than Toby but in fact he had ten years on him. His wife was plain except for the lively gaze from her eyes. She left the *gringo* and her man out front in shade of the "texas."

Sanchez Ortiz rolled black eyes when Toby said who had sent him. As they sat, Ortiz's heavily accented English had a unique habit of mangling words because he thought in Spanish. Of his uncle he said, "My mother used to say her brother would never grow up. But she was wrong. He grew up. He killed men . . . and smiled. Whatever it was he smiled. One time a tarantula bit his left hand. Everyone prayed for his soul . . . soon to depart . . . he smiled."

Toby nodded. "And survived?"

"*Si,* yes. Do you know how old he is?"

"No."

Sanchez Ortiz pointed to some heat-shimmering distant

mountains. "When he was born, they were holes in the ground."

Toby laughed. Sanchez smiled at him. "There is a small stone room out back near the well. You are welcome to stay there as long as you like."

Toby said, "I'll pay," and Sanchez Ortiz looked annoyed. "You are a guest," he said. "Is my uncle coming . . . for some reason?"

"Yes. To teach me how to use a six-gun."

Ortiz looked blank for a moment. "To use a gun? Why?"

"Well, there's a feller coming I got to settle with."

Sanchez crossed himself and muttered, *"Madre de Dios,"* then reverted to English. "I should have known. Friend, I am a peaceable man. I. . . ."

"You won't be part of it," Toby hastily assured Manuel Acosta's nephew. "I'll stay out of your way." He arose. "*Gracias, compañero.* I'll find the stone house by myself."

Sanchez waited until Toby was out of sight, went into the house and told his wife why the *gringo* was here, and who had sent him. She was folding unironed clothing. She flung a garment across the room. "You let him do this to us? The *gringo* is a killer and you allowed this to happen? Sanchez, you are in great measure a disappointment to me!"

Sanchez Ortiz fled the house, wandered to a little hole-in-the-wall *cantina* operated by a very fat Mexican. It was where old men gathered to smoke and talk and young men came to burn scorch from their throats with such things as *aguardienti.* Women did not visit the fat man's saloon. It was a place where men seeking surcease from angry women were safe.

Toby was pleased with the stone hut. For one thing it was cool because of the thick stone walls. For another there was a pallet on the floor — and fleas, but he would not encounter them until nightfall.

He ate at a cafe operated by a straggly-haired woman with two splendid gold teeth in the front of her mouth, and if she ever smiled it would have been something awesome to behold, but she did not smile. No one in Trabajo could remember her ever smiling. The food was peppery and hot enough to the taste to scald the *cajones* off a brass monkey. Toby was becoming accustomed to this kind of food. In fact he was beginning to like it.

The following morning Desdentado arrived. The only way Toby knew this was so was by the sound of a fierce argument in the Ortiz house. One of the disputants talked wetly even in Spanish. But when Acosta came out back he was smiling broadly. He had the six-gun, wrapped in an oily rag, and a gun belt with holster. He had also brought two boxes of bullets — and a bottle of red wine.

When Toby mentioned the argument, Acosta made a disparaging gesture. "My nephew does not use the switch often enough. His wife is a demon. Well, let's get your horse and go riding. I heard by *huaracho* telegraph the prison wagon is expected in Trabajo in less than a week." The tall, thin man rolled his eyes. "You got to learn fast. Come along."

The black man's entire character seemed to change when Toby arrived in Acosta's company. He only referred to the toothless *vaquero* by *"Señor,"* a mark of respect. As Toby and the smiling toothless man were riding through cool morning brilliance west of Trabajo, Acosta laughed, which he did easily anyway, and said, "I tell you something about people, friend. They understand only two things: a man's reputation and fear."

They rode a considerable distance and left the horses in shade, walked behind a pair of enormous corpse-colored rocks. Acosta drank from his bottle, handed Toby the gun wrapped in cloth, the belt and holster, and gestured. "I'll sit in the shade. Do you see those two rocks out ahead? Now don't hurry. Take your time. Put the gun in the holster. Take your time. Draw the pistol and shoot each one of those rocks."

Acosta got comfortable with his back to a rock and nodded. Toby was self-conscious. His draw was clumsy and he missed both rocks.

The toothless, sinewy, dark man grinned and gestured. "Again. Forget I am here. This time, aim."

Toby drew, hesitated to aim, and hit both rocks.

Acosta sipped from the bottle, nodded, and smiled. "Tell me something," he said. "You never drew a gun before?"

"No."

Acosta's dark eyes were bright. It was not common to find a man whose coordination was perfect; Toby's nearly was. He drew the gun in a blur of near-perfect quickness. Acosta had him draw and aim four times in quick succession. Each time the gun seemed almost to spring into his hand. Acosta sipped a little more from the bottle. He was fast because he was also naturally coordinated and he had practiced a lot. Toby had barely begun to practice and he was as fast at drawing and aiming — maybe even faster — than his teacher.

Acosta worked at it until the heat became oppressive, then they returned to Trabajo. Before departing outside his nephew's home, Acosta said, "Go to the room. Practice aiming. Drawing and aiming."

On his way back to the Trinitaria yard Acosta finished the bottle and hid it among some rocks. All the riders were gone but *el jefe*. He was sitting in the barn where it was blessedly cool when Acosta swung down and led his horse inside. He smiled at the *mayordomo.*

Salazar said, "Well, *compañero* . . . ?"

Acosta was off-saddling as he replied. He spoke and smiled at the same time. The smile detracted a little from the words. "He maybe lied about not having handled a pistol before. He is very fast to the draw. As fast as I was at his age. But. . . ." Acosta led the horse out back, corralled it, and returned to drop down on the bench beside Salazar. "Old friend, let me tell you that he can't hit a barn from the inside."

Salazar shrugged. "This is the first day."

Acosta shoved out thin, long legs and sighed. He was slow to reply. "The first day, yes, but I can tell you from experience some men can get out their weapon fast and never learn to shoot straight." Acosta smiled at the ground. "*Jefe,* there are graveyards all over the land of men who were fast to draw and never hit their target. But, yes, it was the first day . . . I should say to you . . . if this Bannion can shoot straight. . . ." Acosta rose, smiled, and walked out into the sunlight.

The *mayordomo* sat a long while in the shadowy coolness of the barn. Eventually he brought in a horse to be saddled. His intention was to ride out, find the *vaqueros,* and work with them the rest of the day. It was a routine matter. He had been doing it for years, but this day he got the horse saddled and bridled when an arrow-straight figure appeared up front, backgrounded by sunlight. He looked across the seat of his saddle. *La patrona* did not often come to the barn like this. He nodded respectfully and waited. It was a very short wait.

She came into the runway where he could see her better and said, "Has Toby gone?"

She had to know Toby had departed. "*Si, señora.*"

"Do you know where he went?"

Salazar cleared his throat. "To Trabajo I think."

"Go at once, find him, and bring him back."

Salazar's eyebrows crawled upwards. He did not move or speak.

She came to the far side of his horse. "*Tía* Maria tried to hang herself."

Salazar stared. "*¿Una curandera, señora?* I know the old woman who. . . ."

"*Jefe,* she needs a doctor, not a medicaster. The nearest one is sixty miles from here."

"Señora, the curandera. . . ."

"Listen to me, *jefe.* The Indian woman who sleeps in the room with her was awakened when Aunt Maria stepped off the chair. She was unable to cut the rope so she screamed. I cut the rope. She was unconscious but the rope was old and stretched. She told us she would do that, but she'd said it other times. Go find Toby. She wants to see her Texan. Do you understand? She is hard to handle. She wants to get up, take a horse, and go find her Texan."

Salazar unlooped the reins, led the horse out into the heat with Lillian Monteverde walking with him. Out there he swung into the saddle. "I'll find him, *Señora,* and I'll bring him back."

Salazar waited until she was back at the big house then went to Acosta's hut, roused the toothless man from a siesta, and asked where Toby was staying in Trabajo. When Acosta told him, Salazar rode away at a kidney-jolting trot. It was too hot to lope any distance.

The toothless man went inside, returned moments later with a tin cup of red wine, and stood on the lee side of his *jacal,* watching the *mayordomo.* He shook his head. Something was wrong. Salazar never pushed an animal in this kind of heat. Desdentado went back inside, put the half-empty tin cup on a makeshift stool beside his bed, lay back, and sighed. In this life more things were wrong than were right, but that was no excuse to trot a horse under a blazing sun.

Salazar did not trot the horse more than a mile. He made it walk. It was his personal mount. He had trained it to be a fast walker. Still, the distance was respectable, so, with nothing else to do as he rode, he thought back many years when he had been a boy and *Tía* Maria had been almost a mother to him. He would cheerfully have pursued that Texan and shot him; and he had not approved when the old *patrón* would not allow Maria to marry her Texan. It had to do with the old *patrón*'s dislike of *gringos,* particularly those from Texas — and *el patrón*'s feeling of shame that his sister would even want to marry that Texan in a church, which was a consecrated place fit only for the faithful and the deserving.

Salazar reached Trabajo when people were taking their siestas, which was the traditional method of avoiding the fierce mid-day heat. Ordinarily they arose just short of dusk, did their chores, and had supper somewhere between eight and nine o'clock.

When Salazar arrived at the house with the wagon canvas to provide shade in front, there was no sign of life. He rode around back to tie his animal in shade, heard someone in the little stone house back there, and approached. The door was half open. Because the small storeroom was made of stone, it was ten degrees cooler inside even with the door open. Salazar looked in. Toby was standing sideways concentrating on the north wall. He made his draw, re-holstered the weapon, sensed something, and faced the doorway. Salazar stepped inside as he dryly said, "I was once told the fastest draws are made only by the Devil's own."

The *mayordomo* went to a bench, sat down, and mopped off sweat. "*La patrona* wants you to come back. Right now. *Tía* Maria tried to hang herself last night."

Toby eased one hip on the corner of an old table. "That's terrible. What can I do?"

Salazar considered a hanging *olla*. They were made of porous clay which kept the water cold to the taste. Before arising to drink he said, "She maybe knew you were leaving. I don't know. What I do know is that she thinks you are her *tejano*." Salazar drank deeply, wiped his chin, and returned to the stool. "I don't know this either, but I think *la patrona* wants you back because the old lady is very bad and she believes seeing you will make her better." Salazar arose. "Where is your horse?"

"At the black man's corral."

"Then let us go."

Toby arose from the edge of the table but was hesitant. "*Jefe,* I'm not a doctor."

"*Si,* I know that. Now will you come?"

Trabajo was still in siesta; only the black man was not; but that was not a total certainty because he was slumped in a cocked-back chair making noise like a shoat caught under a gate. He did not stir even when they led their animals out front before mounting.

On the way Salazar looked solemnly at his companion. "Toby, this man you want . . . have you learned when he will come?"

"He will be in Trabajo in the next few days. This man will also most likely arrive with a gun-guard."

"How do you know this?"

Toby stood in his stirrups. The Trinitaria buildings, although visible, seemed to be floating several feet off the ground in a heat haze.

When Salazar had got no answer to his question he

said, "Desdentado told me you are very quick with a gun."

Toby eased down in the saddle, still squinting ahead to the yard with its clutch of little adobe houses, its immense shade trees, its old corrals and fortress-like barn. Whether he had heard the *mayordomo* or not, when he spoke, his words did not come from the mind, the need for revenge, not even from the natural desire to reach shade. They came from the heart.

"*Jefe,* this is how life should be."

The older man threw Toby a puzzled look. "Waiting to kill a man? Learning to shoot fast and straight?"

Toby looked irritably at his companion. "No! That . . . up ahead . . . the yard, the buildings, the people. Families of them." Toby made an all-encompassing gesture with his rein-free right arm. "Trinitaria is . . . a whole place by itself."

Salazar regarded the younger man as they slouched along, beginning to understand. He too squinted ahead at the yard, but in silence.

When they were in the barn off-saddling, Desdentado came along, sweating like a stud horse but with twinkling eyes which seemed to be watering excessively even for a blazing hot day. He sat on a stool, dragged a limp and soiled sleeve across the wetness of his toothless mouth and said, "So you went after Toby. Why, *jefe?*"

Salazar sounded annoyed when he explained why he had ridden to Trabajo. Acosta made a swift sign of the cross and muttered. "I didn't know. But why should I? An old man with no teeth who does his work without even a woman to make *tortillas.*"

Salazar turned swiftly. In Spanish he said, "Do not whine. Do you feel sorry for yourself? You could have Juanita Flores."

Acosta was wiping both eyes when he replied. "She is too fat. Besides she cooks for you . . . and don't you know, old imbecile, she is in love with you?"

Salazar exploded. Nothing had gone right on this day. "*¡Tonto!* Rider of other people's horses! Skinny because you drink wine instead of eating." He paused, then said in clear contempt, *"Muy matador!"*

Acosta arose and marched stiffly out of the barn. Toby, who had understood a fraction of what Salazar had said, and might have understood more if the *mayordomo* hadn't spoken so fast, led his horse to a stall, closed the door, and kept his back to Salazar. He had an almost overpowering urge to laugh. Something he had learned was that old men were irritable — and funny.

From behind him Salazar said, "Go to the main house." He did not say they would both cross the yard. Toby nodded and returned to the dancing heat.

Salazar sank down on the stool Desdentado had vacated, rolled and lighted a cigarette, shook his head and watched a large hairy spider stalk a fly. The spider crouched. So did the fly who probably thought he could not be caught — if flies thought — and was mistaken. The spider moved so fast when he jumped that the fly did not quite get off the ground before the spider had him.

Salazar felt not a mote of pity. He told the struggling fly in Spanish he was a stupid creature who probably hit his mother, killed the smoke, and went back where heat hit him, tipped down his hat, and walked all the way to his house where the barrel-built woman with the peaches-and-cream complexion was preparing a meal at the corner oven and looked around wearing a wide, shiny smile.

Salazar got a bottle of red wine, tipped a cup half full, sat at the table facing the oven to watch Juanita Flores work. She was fat; everyone including God knew that. She was also caring and jolly — and an incorrigible flirt, not that it mattered; old men could appreciate her for virtues which meant nothing to young men, who were not at all interested in virtues — any kind, the cooking and caring kind, or the other kind.

He said, "Do you know Aunt Maria tried to hang herself last night?"

She nodded with her back to him. "I heard. I also heard you went to find the young *gringo* because she thinks he is her man who went away and never returned."

Salazar sipped wine. It was cool inside the little house. Juanita Flores had a very broad back. "You do not like Manuel Acosta?" he said.

She jiggled food from an iron fry-pan onto a tin plate, brushed hair from above her eyes with the back of a hand, and turned. "He asked you to say that?"

"No."

"Well, he is too thin and his house smells of old sweat and wet rawhide. Also, I have heard stories . . . he has killed many men. A man like that might cut someone's throat when he is full of wine."

Salazar finished the contents of the tin cup and arose to leave. Juanita Flores put both hands on ample hips and spoke sharply. "Where are you going? You didn't smell this food, or maybe you thought I cooked it for the man with no teeth? Come back here, sit down and eat."

Salazar turned in the doorway to regard the woman. "It is too hot. What is it?"

"Food! . . . *Tortilla rellenos carne con chili.* I have been cooking since you rode away."

"How did you know I would come back?"

Juanita Flores rolled her eyes. "Old men always come

back. Young men . . . maybe never. Sit down and eat. I will put more wine in the cup."

He returned to the table, sat down, and regarded the food from an expressionless face. When she brought the re-filled cup, he looked up at her. "You are a bossy woman."

She answered back very quickly. "No. A woman who wants you to eat right and take care of yourself. If a woman is settled, *jefe,* she is not bossy. You understand me?"

The *mayordomo* sat like a statue squinting at Juanita Flores. If God was in His Heaven, had He put those thoughts in Desdentado's mind? If not, why had Desdentado said Juanita Flores loved him?

"Eat, *jefe.* Don't sit there like you've seen a ghost. I will be back later."

As she moved away, she trailed a hand across his shoulder. He waited until she was gone, then reached for the cup of red wine.

Chapter Ten

Schemes and Surprises

The large, low-roofed, rambling main house was cool and shadowy. The custom during each hot season was to open windows at night, close them in the morning and cover them with drapes. It might not have been necessary when walls were adobe three feet thick, but it was tradition and God forfend that anyone should ignore tradition.

The woman who opened the door for Toby was the same sour-faced, squatty Indian woman who had met him at the door once before. She did not speak as she swung the door wide for him to enter, turned her back, and led him through several large rooms furnished with heavy, dark, carved furniture. The house was as silent as a tomb.

La Patrona was sitting at bedside of *Tía* Maria. She arose at once, liquid dark eyes on Toby. There was no trace of the haughtiness.

She took him by the hand to bedside where her sister-in-law's dull look gradually vanished. Her neck was swollen and purple. Clearly, it pained her to move her head, but she raised a wrinkled hand. Toby took it as he sat on the chair Lillian Monteverde had vacated.

The old woman's voice was a croak when she said in English, "They wouldn't let me find you."

He squeezed the chilly fingers. "I've come back."

The old woman's eyes filled with tears and her sister-in-law leaned forward to wipe them with a small handkerchief. The old woman would have twisted away from the younger woman's touch but could not do it without pain, so she closed both eyes. When her sister-in-law pulled back, the old woman said, "I will be fine." She seemed to think a moment before also saying, "It was an accident. I don't know how it happened."

The sour-faced Indian woman made a disparaging grunt which the old woman ignored, but her niece turned and spoke harshly: *"¡Vamos!"*

The Indian woman departed silently.

Tía Maria feebly squeezed Toby's hand. "Tomorrow I will come to our *jacal.* It needs sweeping, and I will cook you a grand meal." She hesitated. "Ruben, the next time let me ride with you."

Toby arose, placed the cold hand atop the counterpane, leaned and kissed the old woman on the forehead. She sighed and closed her eyes.

Out in the large, heavily furnished parlor Lillian Monteverde gazed in long silence at Toby, and then smiled softly. Ignorant maybe, but something very rare, she thought — a man with enough heart to be gentle and understanding. She offered him a meal. He made an excuse — the house, the old woman, even this stunningly beautiful one, made even the thought of eating unpleasant.

She trailed him out into the walled patio. When he would have gone to the gate she said, *"Un momento . . . por favor."*

He turned back, hat in hand. She went to a bench, held both hands in her lap like resting birds. There were things one never did. For example, one never called a retainer by the first name. If she had a struggle about this, it did not show when she said, "Toby, what is there in Trabajo that kept you there?"

She jutted her chin in the direction of a bench. He reluctantly came over and sat down, facing her. "A man's coming to Trabajo I want to see."

Her gaze did not waver. "Why, Toby?"

He turned the hat by its brim in his hands. "I owe him something for a friend of mine."

Her gaze remained fixed. "Money?"

"No ma'am."

"To kill him, Toby . . . ?"

He arose. "What happens when your aunt comes to the little house?"

She sighed and also arose. "She won't be able to. Not for several days. Please don't go back to Trabajo."

He was annoyed. "Thank you for everything, ma'am."

This time when he went to the gate she was silent.

It occurred to him, finally, that the little adobe house Salazar had given him was the *jacal Tía* Maria and her Texan had occupied. When the *mayordomo* appeared in the doorway, Toby asked him if this was so. Salazar nodded, stepped inside, and sat down. "How is the old lady?"

"She looks like hell. Her neck's as big as her head an' it's purple."

El jefe nodded. "The rope was old and rotten. I saw it. I think it would have broken under her weight. I'm not sure but she is very old."

"*Jefe,* who was Ruben?"

"That was the name of her Texan. Ruben Quartermaine."

"Odd name . . . Quartermaine."

Salazar shrugged and straightened up a little. "Desdentado is waiting in his house. I think you got to learn to aim . . . to shoot straight."

After the *mayordomo*'s departure, Toby looked around the room. For a fact it needed cleaning out, but there was no broom. He did not go outside or he would have seen *la patrona* briskly crossing the yard to find *Jefe* Salazar. When she found him out at the corrals, she said, "Don't let Toby go back to Trabajo."

Salazar turned slowly. Her brusqueness had often irritated him. This time he spoke bluntly. "I can't stop him, *señora.*"

"Do you know why he is going there?"

"*Si, señora.* To kill a man who beat a friend of his . . . a little boy . . . so badly that he died."

"Can't you find some work that will keep him busy?"

Salazar shrugged. "For how long, *señora?* No one knows exactly when this man will arrive."

"*Jefe,* for God's sake . . . *do something!*"

A tiny bell was ringing in the back of the *mayordomo*'s head. He had known this woman since she had first come to Trinitaria. Of course, she had changed, mostly since the death of her husband some years back. After his death she had exhibited a degree of iron that had surprised everyone. She surprised him now, not by the words but by the expression on her face. He did not know how to answer her so he fell back on procrastination. What else could a man do?

"*Señora,* I will try, but please remember he is a very strong man . . . not just in the muscles." Salazar read the look in the woman's eyes correctly and was shocked. Toby was only a boy . . . well, in many ways . . . and she was a woman with gray at the temples. He added a little more. "If I can't stop him, then I will see that when he goes back to Trabajo, he will not be alone."

The woman gave Salazar one of her brusque nods and walked away.

The *mayordomo* considered going to Desdentado's house but before he could decide Juanita Flores hailed him from the doorway of his *jacal.* He went in that direction with a furrowed brow and heavy footsteps.

The barrel-shaped woman was in a clean dress and her cheeks were shiny. She waited until he was seated before saying, "Alonzo has asked me to come and cook for him."

The *mayordomo* dully nodded.

Juanita Flores was briefly silent, then with hands on hips confronted him with flashing eyes. "Is this what I get for caring for you, *ingrato?* Are you just such an old man that only horses and cattle occupy your mind?"

Salazar was jarred from his reverie by her loud anger. He said, "Alonzo? That cow-dropping? That *gordo* . . . that big-bellied loafer?"

Juanita Flores stopped her harangue. Her mouth hung open. "You don't want me to do this, then?"

Salazar arose and stamped out of the house. As he was passing through the doorway, he said, "Do what you want . . . you will anyway."

After he was gone, the barrel-shaped woman went after the jug, poured red wine into a cup, and sat at the table to speak softly to herself. "He is yours. Take time. With *el jefe* it will take time because he must believe everything is his idea." She emptied the cup and smiled again. "*¡Los hombres! Muchísimo estúpido . . . y muchísimo grande.*"

Salazar was still nettled when he went to the house of Manuel Acosta and heard the toothless man explaining with temper-edged patience that Toby most likely would not get a second chance. He said, "You are fast enough. I've already told you that. But you must aim before squeezing the trigger, even if you are slower for it. Now, again . . . slower this time and aim squarely at me. Up high. Go . . . *do it!*"

Salazar waited until he heard the firing pin fall on an empty chamber before entering. Desdentado threw up his hands, went to the bottle on a table, tipped red wine into three tin cups, and looked at the *mayordomo.* He spoke Spanish when he said, "Like lightning he is, but he can't aim good enough. If this other man is just a little good with a gun. . . . *Jefe,* I think when the time arrives we should go with this one, otherwise I think he could get hurt."

Toby leathered the six-gun, came to the table for his cup. Although he had been able to pick out an occasional word from the toothless man's statement, he did not understand what exactly had been said.

He grinned at the *mayordomo,* who sat down without grinning back, and raised his cup. When Salazar lowered the cup, he was looking at Manuel Acosta. It was as though Toby was not there. He spoke to Desdentado in Spanish. "The idea is good. You and I will ride with him." The *jefe* then turned to Toby. "The riders are bringing cattle from up north where the feed is eaten down to the dust. Mostly wet cows with hungry calves. You could go meet them and help. Those are not very tame cattle."

Toby drained his cup before asking how long this would take. Salazar, understanding the reason for the question, lied with a clear conscience.

"One day, maybe at the most two days. Don't worry, we will know when the prison wagon arrives."

"How will we know?" Toby asked.

Salazar jutted his chin toward the toothless man. "Manuel will ride to Trabajo today to tell his nephew to come at once and tell us when the wagon arrives."

Desdentado looked round-eyed at the *mayordomo.* "Today?" he asked.

Salazar nodded. "Today, *compañero.* In this heat?"

Salazar left them, less worried about his ability to sidetrack Toby than about what the toothless man had told him. In the *mayordomo*'s mind what had seemed to be a simple, commonplace matter of one man seeking vengeance had turned into something much different. He worried about *la patrona*'s reaction if they brought Toby back dead in a wagon.

Desdentado finally ended the lesson in his residence, told Toby he had to go to Trabajo as the *mayordomo* had said, and added a personal observation.

"It is as hot today as the devil's *chingadero.*"

Toby returned to his own *jacal,* drank from the *olla,* and continued to practice with the perfectly balanced Colt of Manuel Acosta.

Outside women screamed at children; some wilting, runty chickens stood forlornly in barn shade with wings extended; and horses in the corral divided their time between the stone trough and the shade of a large old tree which sagacious corral-builders now long in their graves had left standing for that precise purpose.

The *vaqueros* arrived in late afternoon on tired horses to explain to the *mayordomo* that with considerable difficulty they had managed to get the cattle within about a mile and a half of the yard. They also told him there was a cow with only one horn which had maggots in the other horn. How she had broken the horn off the riders had no idea, but they assured Salazar that she was not only fast, and crazy from torment, but would charge — even at a man on horseback.

The riders cared for their animals and scattered among their little houses. Before they had left the barn, Salazar told them Toby would ride with them in the morning.

They had accepted it without comment. They liked this *gringo.* He was different from all the other patronizing, know-it-all *gringos* they had encountered.

Dusk arrived slowly. It was past nine o'clock before it shaded away toward night. It was cooler too, not much, but at least the pitiless sun was gone. This was the special time of day when the riders, their wives and children sat outside, talked, drank red wine, smoked, watched the children, the dogs among the children, and those with the gift played guitars and accompanied the music with *canciones,* usually about tragedies, occasionally marches which, in the most popular of the songs, extolled both cockroaches and marijuana.

Toby was outside when someone said something he did not understand and nudged a companion. They both looked in the direction of the *mayordomo*'s house. He was sitting on a bench with the barrel-built woman. She was animated, using both arms as she spoke. The *mayordomo* sat forward, looking gravely at the ground. One of the *vaqueros* whispered something to his friend, and they both laughed. An old woman using the same bench turned indignantly and told them in Spanish that they had disgusting minds, that she had known the *mayordomo* from childhood. When he sat like that he had something more worrisome to ponder than what they thought. They had not known she had heard them talking.

Toby waited until dark to go out back and take an all-over bath in the stone trough, then to sit in weak moonlight until he was dry and got dressed. Inside the *jacal* it was still warm; not hot, no structure with mud walls three feet thick was ever hot or, with only the smallest of fires in the corner oven, ever got cold.

He bedded down, lay a long time with both arms under his head staring into the darkness. This was the time of memories, of which he now had more than a few.

Where were Buttons and Molly? They were older; so was he, almost twenty-one. Where was that bull-necked foreman of the rail gang named Sheuermann whom the paymaster had renamed Sherman? Where was Mr. Roberts? Probably a little more stooped but still working.

He was beginning to recall the Dutchman in whose shed he and Buttercup had been happy in their secret place when he fell asleep.

He was awakened in a world of utter stillness and darkness. He gently felt the pallet on his left side, felt again, then did not move as he put both arms atop the blankets as stiff as a ramrod staring up where blackness hid the ceiling. For a long time he did not move, not until a soft, raspy voice said, "Ruben . . . ?"

Tía Maria for God's sake!

He managed a soft, "Yes? How did you get here? You should be in bed over at the big house."

"I was over there but I knew you would be here, in our own place. I walked. Something hurts my neck. Do I sound hoarse to you?"

She raised a thin old arm and gently placed it across his chest as he was trying to think how he should answer.

"You had an accident . . . ?"

"Were you there?"

"No, but I was told. Aunt Maria. . . ."

"I am not your aunt. I am not even Lillian's aunt. Why don't you call me *querida* the way you did before you left?"

He hadn't the faintest idea what *querida* meant, but it was easy to pronounce. "*¡Querida!*"

"*Querida Maria. Mi amor.* No . . . you don't like it. In English, then. You are my love, Ruben. As long as

I live. I missed you so much."

The old woman sat up; he could hear her fumbling with her clothes and had a terrifying thought, but she leaned across him, holding something.

"Enrique. The year before the snake bit him. Can you see him?"

He couldn't even see her clearly. "No. In the morning. . . ."

She wiggled free of the blankets and went groping for a candle. Finding something to light it with required more scrambling and groping, but she said, "Ahhh," and moments later the candle flickered to light.

Toby was getting into his trousers when she returned and leaned over. By candlelight she looked frightening, hair askew, neck swollen and discolored, wrinkles showing like old lace-work. Only her dark eyes glistened as she held the candle in front of a photograph.

"Your son, Ruben. He has your mouth and chin. Isn't he a beautiful boy? I called him Ruben, for you, but not in front of my brother. He called him 'that boy.' Ruben, take the picture. It will be daylight soon. I'll make a fire in the stove, make breakfast for you."

She left him holding the picture. He could hear her bumping things, muttering until she found the stove and once more a smoking sulfur match was ignited. He could see her feeling for kindling. It was as though a genuine witch had materialized before him.

Toby arose, finished dressing, put the photograph of Enrique on the table with the candle in front, and straightened as she turned.

"He was such a treasure to me, Ruben. A good boy." Her voice faltered. "My brother would not have him in the house. He had to live here with me. Everyone loved him. Sit down. I will tell you about him as you eat. There isn't much to make a meal of. I'll get things from the house." She stopped talking, turned and looked steadily at him. "I never blamed you. It was something you had to do but . . . would you tell me . . . why, Ruben? I wasn't a good wife to you? I thought I was. I tried. Was it my brother? Because he didn't like you? No, it was I, wasn't it. Tell me, Ruben."

Her voice was still raspy, but now it became unsteady. She was crying and, although he could not see tears, he could hear sniffles. He sat like a stone, candlelight showing faintly on his face. He had no idea what to say or do. He moved the picture slightly farther from the candle.

She said, "He was beautiful, Ruben. You would have been so proud. So straight and handsome. So full of laughter and smiles. He liked everyone . . . well, nearly everyone . . . people loved him."

She had to stop, bend far over with a cloth to her face. The fire in the stove brightened. Dawn was arriving in the hazy east. Someone called from the barn or near it. Toby recognized the answering voice: the *mayordomo*.

He was unable to distinguish words until he heard a woman's voice, sharp and piercing.

"*¡Jefe!* There . . . in that house with the door open . . . a bright fire."

Chapter Eleven

One Old Cow

Lillian Monteverde entered the little house leaving the *mayordomo* in the doorway. She threw Toby one glance, then went to the old woman and, with an arm around her shoulders, led her outside. There she told Salazar to return the old woman to the main house. As he nodded and moved to obey, Lillian Monteverde reëntered the *jacal* where Toby had extinguished the light.

For a moment she simply looked at him, then said, "The Indian woman sleeps like a rock."

He nodded. "I sure wasn't expectin' her, ma'am."

La patrona went to the table and sat down. "I don't know what to say. The Indian woman will go." She raised her face to him. "I'm sorry, Toby."

He remained standing across the table from her. "She's harmless, ma'am. But she give me a start. I was asleep. She climbed into the blankets. . . ." He paused. "It caught me plumb off guard an' about half asleep."

La patrona looked at the hands in her lap. "I can lock her in the room. I've thought of that. But. . . ."

"She's your kin, ma'am. You can't do that to your kin. Bein' locked up does somethin' to a person's spirit. Even someone . . . like her."

Lillian Monteverde's frustration made her tone sharp when she said, "What, then? Let her wander beyond the house? Let her come back to this place? Let her delusion about you continue?"

"No ma'am. Give her this little house. Find another old woman to live with her, take care of her, mind that she don't go wandering off."

"And you?" the beautiful woman said. "Every time she sees you. . . ."

"I'll leave, Miz Monteverde. I figured to when I rode off the last time. With me gone, *Tía* Maria will. . . ."

She stared at him. He was so dumb — so naive. "Toby, if you leave . . . don't you understand? She will think her Texan has deserted her again. One of the times when she tries to kill herself, she will succeed. *¿Comprende?*"

He went after the jug, filled two tin cups half full, set one in front of her, sat opposite her with the other one, and said, "Yes, I understand. Well, I tried to help an' it wasn't no good. Now then, *you* tell *me* what to do about her."

Their discussion ended when Salazar appeared in the doorway. "The riders are ready," he said, looking at Toby.

Lillian Monteverde arose, pushed past the *mayordomo* who turned from watching her briskly walking in the direction of the main house to gaze thoughtfully at Toby. "It is time to work those wild cattle."

Toby dropped his old hat atop a mass of unshorn hair and hurried to the barn area where *vaqueros* were waiting. None of them spoke, but they smiled. They already knew what had happened. In a place like Trinitaria or any other of the semi-feudal immense *ranchos* of the Southwest, the only way to keep a secret was to tell it first. They all knew about *Tía* Maria, had known about her for years. What they had recently discovered about the old woman and the *gringo* was "of an immense novelty."

* * * * *

Toby had a lesson in handling wild cattle. The riders, including Desdentado and the *mayordomo,* rode easterly for three hours, then went northward for more than another hour before making their final alteration of course which was southeast on an angling westerly tangent until they came in from behind the longhorns. This achieved a purpose: the cattle had been watching southerly, the direction they had last seen the *vaqueros.* This appearance from the north kept the cattle surprised and motionless for several minutes.

Toby saw one cow drop her head and paw. She only had one horn. It was on her right side. Someone sang out to the *mayordomo.* He had also seen the half-crazy fighting cow.

They got the band moving — at a leisurely but steady walk. Anything faster, any unnecessary noise like shouting, could set the cattle into a wild, scattering, headlong run. Some of those razor-backs could outrun a good horse. The animals went along peacefully enough as long as the riders did not come too close, did not crowd them.

A lean, very dark *vaquero* smiled as he came up to ride stirrup with Toby. With considerable positioning of lips he said, "It is a nice today."

Toby agreed with a straight face. "Very nice."

Having succeeded in English his first time, the *vaquero* spoke next with more confidence. "You be a mare. I be a horse. My name is what? . . . Ignacio."

Toby shook the extended hand as he said, "My name is Toby Lincoln."

"Ah . . . Lincoln! . . . he lives in . . . *Guazington?*"

Someone up ahead was shouting and gesturing. Ignacio swung easterly in a rush to cut back some animals — called bunch-quitters — who were trying to reach a dense thicket of desert thornpin. If they reached it and got deeply enough into the brush, they could not be roped and dragged out, and there were no dogs along. Trinitaria's riders scorned the use of dogs.

It was a narrow race, but Ignacio flashed across the front of the cattle, turned back, and swung his coiled lariat as he passed in front again. He did not turn the bunch-quitters back, but he delayed them until other riders arrived. They drove the cattle back to the herd.

Toby could see the yard with its large old trees and also the sprawling main house. Cattle and drovers were drooping. The sun had made its pitiless march toward the meridian, and now hung there, emanating heat in all directions accompanied by a shimmering of the land which made things appear to be not on the ground but slightly above it.

The tormented, single-horned cow and her thin, leggy calf plodded along, heads down and mouths open.

The *mayordomo* stood in his stirrups and waved with his right arm. He then turned westward at a walk and did not look back. He knew the other riders would be following.

It did not take as long to reach the yard this time, only maybe a third of the time it had taken to surround the razor-backs earlier. When they led their animals into the cool mud barn to be cared for, that *vaquero* who had practiced his English on Toby led his horse out back, carrying a bucket. At the trough he scooped the bucket full and dumped it over the horse's back. He did this three times before turning the animal into the corral. The horse promptly turned three times before dropping down to roll, first to one side, then to the other side. More riders led their horses out and used the same bucket the first man had used.

The *mayordomo* saw Toby watching, came over to explain. He said, "Taste the sweat where your saddle sat."

Toby stared. "What?"

Salazar ran a finger over the horse's back and touched the finger to his tongue.

"Do it," he ordered.

Toby obeyed.

Salazar then said, "Salty, no? Now, if you turn a horse out into a hot place with little sun without washing his back, the sweat dries, the salt don't. It scalds the back. You understand?"

Toby nodded. Every day he was learning something.

Before leading his own animal to the trough Salazar made a scorning remark: "Cowboys! Do you know what a cowboy is, Toby? He is a man who knows a little about cattle and nothing about horses."

Toby was the last rider to rinse off his horse. The others had scattered among their little residences. Only Desdentado lingered to drink and go into the shade beside the *mayordomo* to whom he said, "I told my nephew."

Salazar grunted with a nod as Toby joined them.

"How about water for those cattle?" Toby asked.

Salazar answered shortly, "There is a spring west of here. In a few days we'll take them there and leave them." When Toby frowned, Salazar added, "These are desert cattle. For a hundred years they have learned to go without drinking, sometimes for almost a week." He grinned at Toby's expression, said something in Spanish, and leaned at the trough to splash water over his face, his head, and the front of his shirt.

Desdentado left them. Salazar watched the skinny, toothless man making a bee-line for his *jacal.* Salazar said nothing, but shook his head. Desert longhorns were not the only creatures on Trinitaria who could go a long time without water.

They entered the barn. It was close to siesta time. The yard was empty; the huts were quiet; even the horses dozed in tree-shade.

Salazar rolled a smoke while sitting on an old bench. He offered Toby the sack and papers. Toby shook his head which made the older man offer a comment.

"The things which don't cost much are sometimes the real pleasures."

A small rooster with gaudy feathers, following a small hen, came into the barn. She carried her head low in a harassed manner. The rooster moved swiftly. Salazar sighed. He told the rooster in Spanish it was too hot.

The pursuit continued until the rooster cornered the hen who offered no further resistance, as the rooster treaded her back until she squatted. The hen did not move. The rooster had triumphed; he had won her compliance. He fluttered his feathers, clawed her twice, then stopped.

Salazar addressed him, "I told you, it is too hot."

Evidently it was because the gaudy little rooster left the squatting hen to go deeper into shade, looking for bugs.

The older man finished his smoke, killed it, and strolled to the front barn opening, for which there was no door. He tipped down his hat and pinched his eyes nearly closed. He should have gone to his hut to sleep away the worst of the heat, but he had a reason for avoiding the *jacal.*

Toby said, "How do you handle those cattle when it is time to make the cut?"

The older man was squinting in the direction of the main house and ignored Toby's question as he straightened up.

"That damned Injun. Look, it is *Tía* Maria . . . again!"

The old woman had a *rebozo* over her head as she got clear of the house, paused, possibly for bearings, then shuffled in the direction of the barn, leaving tiny dust-puffs behind each step. Toby couldn't believe it. Not after what *la patrona* had said earlier about watching the old woman more closely.

Salazar shook his head. "You had better not go to your house. Let her get past, then I'll go tell *la patrona* she is loose again."

The old woman abruptly stopped, raised her head, looking northward. Both men at the barn also turned and Salazar ripped out a fierce oath in Spanish. That one-horned, crazy cow with a stringy calf following was entering the yard. She had perhaps scented the trough. Just as likely, being contrary by nature, she had left the others for no reason, but whatever the purpose she stopped in speckled tree-shade to watch the old woman.

It was doubtful whether *Tía* Maria could have got back to the main house even if the idea had occurred to her. The cow had dropped her head. She pawed, throwing dust over her back and in the face of her calf.

Toby yelled for the old woman to run. *Tía* Maria did not seem to hear; she stood like a statue, watching the cow with one horn.

Salazar swore again, this time in English, because he did not have his pistol. Working rangemen rarely wore sidearms; they were heavy and got in the way. Salazar sprung his legs to run forward and at least knock the old woman to the ground where the crazy cow might be unable to hook her.

It may have been the *mayordomo*'s movement in the barn doorway; it could just as easily have been because the cow was going to charge anyway; but, as Salazar yelled at the old woman and ran toward her, the cow charged.

She had to pass within about thirty feet of the barn opening where Toby stood. She was bony, possibly the result of loss of appetite after the maggots got into the horn cavity, or just as likely because this was her seventh or eighth calf; but with no spare weight she left tree-shade with unusual speed even for a longhorn. Toby had moments to do something. He also had no gun. He crouched, hoped when he judged the cow's speed he was correct. When she was close enough, he sprang out of the barn, running to intercept her. The cow did not heed him. Her full attention was upon the old woman wearing a black *rebozo.* She had to have seen Salazar trying to reach the old woman, but what she did not see, evidently, even though she had perfect side vision, was the young man on a collision course with her left shoulder, the side where there was no horn.

Toby struck the cow running as hard as he could. He threw up both arms before the collision. She had two legs off the ground when he struck her. His solid weight knocked the cow sideways. She fought to hold her balance, failed, and fell to both knees. When she finally saw Toby, he was less than ten feet away and approaching. The cow was too slow getting off her knees. Toby kicked her as hard as he could under the ear on the right side. Maggots and pus sprayed in all directions. The cow staggered, refused to go down, and hung there, a hundred feet from the old woman and the *mayordomo.*

From outside the gate of the main house someone called to Toby. "Get out of the way!"

He saw *la patrona* raising a rifle. He stepped in front of the dazed cow. *La patrona* swore at him.

"You damned fool! *Get out of the way!*"

Toby started walking. He kept the cow between them. He reached Lillian Monteverde, wrenched the rifle from her, swung it as hard as he could against the mud wall of the patio, smashing it irretrievably, and dropped it at her feet as he glared.

Two *vaqueros* with drover's whips appeared to drive the cow away. Salazar held *Tía* Maria motionless as they both stared toward the main house where Lillian Monteverde was white to the hairline with shock.

Toby was breathing hard. His side hurt where years back he had been beaten by a larger boy. There was sweat darkening his shirt. As they faced each other, he finally loosened a little, opened the gate, and jerked his head for her to enter. She moved like a sleepwalker. They stood in blessed shade with flower-bloom fragrance tinting the air. She stared at him as though she could not believe what he had done.

"Years back I found a hurt an' starved Injun colt. It was like that old cow. It couldn't help itself. I hid in a farmer's barn with it. I fed it. Have you ever loved an animal? One day I came back to the barn . . . the homesteader had shot my colt."

Lillian Monteverde went to a bench and sat down. She looked up at Toby without speaking. He tried to think of something to ease her anger.

"*Tía* Maria is safe. I'm sorry about the gun."

He left her standing there, nodded to the *mayordomo* and the old woman as he passed, went to his hut, and drank from the *olla* until fresh sweat burst out all over him.

The following morning with the sun climbing, Sanchez Ortiz arrived on horseback. The prison wagon was in Trabajo. It had arrived some time in the night.

Three riders trailed Desdentado's nephew in the direction of the village. One twisted in the saddle, saw the woman like a stone carving outside the patio gate, watched her for a moment, then sat forward. The *mayordomo* would not have thrown a salute to *la patrona* if it cost him his soul for not doing it.

Acosta said nothing until they had Trabajo in sight, then he told Toby to draw and aim from the back of a horse. Salazar spoke in rancorous Spanish to the toothless man. "How does that make sense? Do you think this Bannion will be riding a horse?"

"No," Acosta shot back. "But this one should be prepared for what might happen. Not just now, old crank, but as he gets older."

"*If* he gets older," Salazar said in Spanish.

As usual Trabajo was lethargic. Ordinarily desert communities were busy in the morning, doing whatever had to be done out of doors before the heat arrived. Trabajo began preparing for the heat before it arrived.

There really was so little commerce the residents of the village had no particular reason to do more than they did, which was gossip, loaf, and anticipate whatever arrived in the village from other areas. The prison wagon was not the first most of the residents had seen, but it was the first in a very long time, especially such a wagon from Colorado, many miles north.

The constable-barman had been as astonished as his patrons at the saloon when the wagon arrived. Because he anticipated a visit from the men who had arrived with the wagon, he had questions for them, the first of which was the matter of jurisdiction. When the strangers entered the saloon in soiled and rumpled blue uniforms, the barman — and his customers — were waiting.

One of the strangers in their look-alike suits, the driver, was a thin, wiry man, lined and graying with the sly features of a fox. He ordered a drink, ignored everyone until he had downed it, and had struck the bartop for a refill.

His companion was a bull-necked, thick man of no more than average height whose slit of a mouth had a downward droop. He had coarse features and surly eyes. They were both armed but the burly man also carried a sawed-off shotgun in the crook of one arm. Before this individual called for whiskey, he asked where the local peace officer was. The barman took his time serving them before saying, "I'm constable."

The unpleasant thick-set man was blunt. "What's your name?"

"Pat Everson . . . what's yours?"

"Jack Bannion." As the burly man answered, he unbuttoned his coat, fished inside, brought forth two limp papers, and put them on the bar. He said, "Read 'em, Mister Everson," and reached for the small glass of whiskey.

The barman spread both papers atop the bar, groped for a pair of glasses, let them slide down his nose, and leaned with a puckered brow. He read both papers, which were identical in content except for names. The silent customers waited for the barman to fold his spectacles, pocket them, and stare at the man with the short-barreled shotgun. "I figured someone from New Mexico would come for them two."

Bannion pushed the jolt glass aside, still with the scatter-gun in the bend of his arm. "Now you know better, don't you?" he said. "When you notified the New Messico authorities you had them two in your jail, Colorado already had a warrant out for them an' a bounty. Did you ever see an extradition order, Mister Everson?"

Bannion's tone stung the barman, so he lied. "I've seen 'em before. You come a hell of a distance just for a couple of cow thieves, Mister Bannion."

"Jeff here has, Mister Everson. I'm a prison guard. When the order come to bring them two back, I come along because the regular guard was down with the summer complaint." Bannion paused. "How do you say the name of this place?"

"Tra-bah-ho. You never been in New Mexico before, Mister Bannion?"

"No sir, an' what I've seen of it, it won't bother me a bit if I never see it again. Mister Everson, me'n Jeff would like to load them rustlers and head back . . . if you don't mind."

Bannion's cranky bearing had alienated everyone in the saloon including the man who owned the place. The driver, Jeff, smiled slyly, drank, and seemed disinterested in everything but fortifying himself for the long first lap of the return trip.

Bannion was only unique in one way — aside from his shotgun, he wore a standard shell belt and holstered six-gun. The driver wore a belt without loops and the pistol in his holster was a double-action weapon. Unlike Colt six-guns which had to be cocked for each shot, the fox-faced man's sidearm could be fired repeatedly simply by pulling the trigger.

Most of the men in the saloon had seen such guns; none had ever owned one, primarily because such a newfangled contraption was not something a man wanted to rely on if staying alive meant knowing a gun wouldn't jam.

The saloonman and his customers were neutral toward the driver, who wore a perpetual slight smile and ignored everything but getting fortified. In fact, as the conversation between the barman and Bannion wound down, the driver put some silver on the counter and pointed to a bottle on the backbar, which Everson got for him, scooped up the coins, and returned his attention to the burly, bullying man with the scatter-gun.

Everson re-read the extradition papers, folded them very carefully, and offered Bannion a false smile as he said, "I'll get the key," and passed through a door in the rear wall.

The saloon had about as many men in it as it had on Saturday nights. Most were not drinking; it was too early in the day; but everyone of them had formed an opinion of the strangers as they sat in silence waiting for the barman to return with his key to the *juzgado.*

Bannion, thick shoulders hunched, leaned while drumming his fingers on the bartop. Neither Bannion nor the others paid the slightest attention to the tall, skinny Mexican whose mouth fell inward when he pushed into the room.

He moved like a cat, found an unoccupied chair at a poker table, sat down, and did not blink during his lengthy appraisal of the men in dark uniforms. The only thing that interested the toothless man was the burly man's armament. He had anticipated the six-gun — not the sawed-off shotgun. There wasn't a weapon on earth which could match a shortened, double-barreled shotgun for killing ability at close range.

When the barman returned, he nodded and led the way out of the saloon in the direction of the jailhouse. Behind, patrons trooped outside, stood quietly watching as the barman unlocked the jailhouse and entered, followed by the pair of men in dark uniforms.

Among the spectators in front of the saloon was the tall, lean Mexican. He sifted through the small crowd and disappeared down an alley.

Chapter Twelve

A Bright Clear Morning

The *mayordomo* listened, then said, "Manuel, go across the road, stay on the north side of the jailhouse so you will be behind them."

Desdentado nodded.

Salazar faced Toby. "Now listen to me. I will go over in front of the store. Manuel will be behind them. I will be in front. You understand?"

Toby frowned. "That's a bushwhack. You two stay out of it. He don't mean anythin' to you . . . he means a lot to me."

Salazar and Desdentado exchanged a look before the *mayordomo* addressed Toby again. "There are two of them. Maybe some of the fools in the village will make trouble. You are one man. Stay out of the range of that shotgun. You understand? Call him when you're ready, but if he tries to use the shotgun. . . ."

As the older man shrugged, Desdentado broadly smiled, showing a wide wet mouth without teeth. He gave Toby a light pat on the arm and turned away.

The *mayordomo* had one more admonition. "The other one carries one of those guns you don't have to cock after each bullet. Leave that one to us." He reverted to Spanish. "It is said, vengeance belongs to *Espirito Santo.* He will repay, *compañero,* today. He seeks vengeance through you. You are His instrument. Wait five minutes after I leave, then go."

Toby waited in the alley where he could not see the roadway for what he assumed had to be sufficient time for Salazar to be in place, then crossed up through a dog-trot between two buildings, halted to look southward where the door of the jailhouse was open, and leaned in cool shade on the east side of the roadway. Once, he made a flashing draw of Manuel Acosta's customized, perfectly balanced Colt, then he briefly looked elsewhere. He saw the toothless man on the north side of the *juzgado*. He leaned to look in the direction of the store but, because it had a recessed doorway, he could not see the *mayordomo*.

Moments passed on leaden feet. It was still cool but the sun was beginning to reach the upper parts of the buildings on the west side of the road.

An old Mexican came up the middle of the road leading a burro whose expression of patient resignation was perpetual. There were ropes on the burro. The old man was going after wood faggots which he would sell in the village.

A solitary woman carrying a net shopping bag walked southward. She was tall, erect, and very dark. Toby held his breath as she crossed the roadway on an angling course in the direction of the store. If the men emerged from the jailhouse, she would be in the line of fire.

He was sweating, not so much with fear as with impatient anticipation. He thought he was distant enough not to be hit by scatter-gun pellets. Sawed-off shotguns had a very limited range, but they spewed pellets in an ever widening pattern before they lost momentum.

The woman reached Toby's side of the roadway, threw him an expressionless glance, and a short distance farther along disappeared inside the store.

Desdentado removed his hat, gestured with it as he wiped his forehead, resettled the hat, and moved very cautiously toward the end of the wall. Here he would have an excellent view of the men he had heard inside the jailhouse stop talking and begin moving.

Toby saw the signal, breathed deeply, and straightened up.

The first man out of the jailhouse was Everson, the saloonman. He was followed by the wiry man who wore the double-action revolver. This one swept the roadway north and south with a wary expression.

The men who came out next were in chains. They were young, Mexican, and clearly troubled, evident even from as far off as Toby was watching.

He loosened his stance with both eyes fixed on the jailhouse door. The last man to emerge had a shotgun in the crook of one arm. He also had a holstered Colt on the left side.

Toby shot a quick look elsewhere, up and down the roadway, then stepped from shadows into sunshine, walking without haste in the direction of the men across the roadway.

Everson turned to speak briefly with Bannion then struck out on a diagonal course for his place of business, clearly having done his duty and anxious to be shed of the whole business. He did not recognize the muscular younger man until they were less than fifteen feet apart, one moving northward, the other passing southward. Everson's step faltered; his eyes sprang wide. Toby did not look at him. Everson let the younger man pass, then turned. Someone hissed loudly from a doorway and told him fiercely to get out of the road. Everson was never afterward able to say who had warned him, but the man in the recessed doorway had sounded deadly serious. Everson widened his stride, reached the front of his saloon, turned and watched the younger man stop less than a hundred feet from the four men in front of the jailhouse. Everson heard every word Toby said although Toby did not raise his voice.

"Bannion!"

All four men in front of the jailhouse turned at the same time. Toby still did not raise his voice. "Bannion, you murderin' son-of-a-bitch, step clear of them other fellers."

Bannion visibly tightened. "Lincoln?"

"Yes. Toby Lincoln. You remember Abel?"

The burly man's tongue made a swift circuit of his lips. He did not answer; in fact, he did not utter a sound. He was making a fast judgment. If he started to swing the shotgun down to hold it with both hands, cock it and fire, if the man he was facing was even average with a belt-gun, he could get off at least one shot first.

If he dropped the scatter-gun and went for his hip-holster, he would also lose time. His tongue made another circuit of his lips before he said, "That kid died because he had lung fever. Had it real bad."

Toby cut this short. "I'm goin' to kill you for what you done to Abel. He was just a little boy. He shouldn't even have been there. Bannion, I don't give a damn whether you use your weapons or not, I'm goin' to kill you."

The wiry, slight man moved his right arm. From the north corner of the building someone cocked a six-gun. No one looked around but the wiry man very slowly raised his right hand away from the double-action pistol.

A gaudily-plumed small rooster came into the roadway clucking several runty hens to follow. The rooster made the only sound for what seemed ages.

Toby spoke again, in the same ordinary voice. "You better do somethin', you son-of-a-bitch, because I'm goin' to shoot whether you do or not."

Bannion watched Toby the way an eagle would watch a rattlesnake — wanting to make the kill, but wary. He said, "I'll lean the scatter-gun aside, then we can settle it with pistols."

From across the road in doorway shadow a harsh-toned voice said, "If he moves, kill him. Go ahead . . . lean your shotgun aside."

The wiry man was white in the face. He looked over in Salazar's direction but all he saw was a tall, erect, dark woman emerge from the store with a knit shopping bag on one arm.

Bannion did not search for the speaker. His eyes were fixed on Toby. "I'll put the shotgun against the wall. All right?"

Toby almost imperceptibly nodded.

Bannion moved, half turned to lean and put his double-barreled weapon aside, looked over his shoulder and sprang sideways clawing for his holstered weapon.

Toby was faster. His first bullet hit the wiry man, Jeff, squarely in the center of the chest. Jeff was knocked against the pair of prisoners, who caught him and flung him away.

Bannion got off a fast shot. It was too low but it drew blood and nearly upset Toby when the bullet tore through his leg. He had to fight to hold steady as he fired again. This time his aim was better. He hit Bannion high in the right chest. The burly man was punched sideways and faltered. Toby fired one more time. Bannion did not stagger. He fell in a heap with blood coming from his mouth, but only briefly; a heart that is not pumping circulates no blood. Toby's second shot had drilled Bannion through the middle of the chest.

For five seconds no one moved; then Salazar came from his doorway and Desdentado moved into sight. They pushed Toby to the ground. Salazar used his belt to stop most of the bleeding from the wounded leg, and Acosta saw the black man among the small crowd of onlookers who had appeared from nowhere and told him to hitch a wagon and be quick about it.

They carried Toby to the general store and under the stare of the proprietor placed him atop a counter. Everson, the saloonman, appeared, told the storekeeper to get bandaging cloth and disinfectant. When these things were provided, Salazar as well as the saloonman were working on the gun-shot leg. Desdentado said to the storekeeper, "Do you know what size pants he wears? His pants are torn and bloody. Get them! An' a shirt . . . an' boots. *¡Pronto!*"

People appeared in the doorway but did not enter the building. One old man, as dark as ancient leather, removed his hat to expose a full thatch of snow-white hair. He mumbled a prayer in Spanish and departed.

Toby's leg was numb. Everson assured him the numbness would not last long. When the pain arrived, he would need whiskey, and offered to go after a bottle. Salazar looked sourly at the saloonman. In his long lifetime he had never found whiskey capable of alleviating pain unless a man drank much of it, in which case his head and stomach bothered him for two days far worse in most cases than whatever he had used the whiskey to alleviate.

Toby's numbness was indeed fleeting. It came from shock and disbelief. He remembered being hit, but at that moment and for several moments afterwards he had been conscious of one thing to the exclusion of pain and everything else. Not until he saw Bannion go down, half in the roadway, half in jailhouse shadow, was he willing to accept the fact that he had been shot. It did not begin to hurt until they placed him atop the counter and Salazar worked on the gory gash with cloth and disinfectant.

It required a singular effort to force the bleeding to stop. When the black man arrived with a wagon, they loaded Toby into it. The black man'd had enough presence of mind to pitch hay onto the bed of the wagon. It was a considerate act but not a very satisfactory one. His wagon was for light drayage and had no springs.

Manuel Acosta remained behind to lead the horses home. He also rifled the pockets of the dead men, appropriating their money and weapons. Alive they had meant no more to Desdentado than exterminable varmints; dead they were simply gun-shot bodies that had to be put into the ground quickly. Gun-shot bodies filled rapidly with gas. Any kind of dead meat on the south desert had to be disposed of very quickly, particularly during the hot time of the year.

When the wagon finally reached the Trinitaria yard, Toby's pain felt like a steady-burning, red-hot branding iron had been pressed into the flesh. He had lost consciousness once half way back, and now did a second time when they lifted him out of the wagon, carrying him to his pallet in the *jacal.*

The *mayordomo* went after Juanita Flores. On the way back the woman said, "*Jefe,* you are too old for this. You look terrible."

Salazar's retort was predictable. "My mother said to me when I was a child that I would never win a beauty prize. Too old! Ignacio is younger?"

Juanita Flores quickened her step, ignoring the *mayordomo* as she entered Toby's hut, pushed the black man and others aside, sank to her knees, leaned to examine the gory leg, and turned quickly to face Salazar. "Get the doctor!"

He frowned. "Sixty miles from here? You crazy woman, he will be dead before I ride half the distance?"

She reddened. "At the house! *La patrona* sent for him four days ago, after the cow tried to attack Maria, who is very ill. Close your mouth! It is the truth. The doctor is with Aunt Maria . . . and his friend, the priest from Mission Dolores! Go, you imbecile."

Salazar turned; several onlookers nodded. He left the hut, muttering to himself.

The woman who opened the door to Salazar was a youngish Indian, not fat yet but with obvious signs that she soon would be. She smiled, which the sour-faced woman who had cared for *Tía* Maria had never done. He removed his hat and asked for *la patrona.* The woman widened her hold on the door as she said she would bring back *la patrona* who was with the doctor in her sister-in-law's room.

Salazar did not enter the house. He turned back as far as a bench where he was sitting, hat in both hands, when Lillian Monteverde appeared, expecting the worst. She said, "Toby?"

"Si, señora."

"You brought him back in a wagon?"

"Yes. He is wounded in the upper leg."

"Alive?" she said, her face losing most of its dour expression.

Salazar gazed at her; he had just told her Toby had been wounded — not killed. "Wounded, *patrona.* He suffered a lot. He lost a lot of blood, but yes, he is alive." Salazar stood up. "He killed them both."

"Both, *jefe?* Never mind. I'll bring the doctor."

Salazar softly said, "*Tía* Maria . . . ?"

"It is her throat. The swelling got worse. She can't eat, but she can drink watered wine." The stunning woman's gaze slid away from the *mayordomo*. "The doctor said . . . she is very old and there is nothing he can do. She will die."

"*Señora,* I am very sorry."

Lillian Monteverde accepted that. "I'll bring the doctor."

She left him standing in the patio. He watched the door close behind her. One time, as a young man, he had heard a *gringo* say that trouble does not travel alone; it always has company.

He returned to the *jacal* where only Desdentado and Juanita Flores remained. Manuel had a cup of red wine he was tipping past the gray lips of the wounded man. As Salazar entered, they all looked at him. He told them what *la patrona* had said about the doctor. Desdentado emptied what remained in the cup in two swallows, then put a hard look on the *mayordomo*. "Did you see that? He shot them both! This man who couldn't shoot straight."

Salazar was tempted to say it had been either an accident or a miracle, when Desdentado showed one of his pink-gum smiles and departed.

Juanita Flores had her head cocked slightly when she asked a question. "*Tía* Maria, *jefe* . . . ?"

He shrugged, went to stand over Toby, looking down. "The doctor will arrive, *compañero*. He can give you something for the pain."

Toby ignored that to ask a question. "The old lady is dying?"

Salazar shrugged. In his long lifetime he had known of several dying people who did not die. "It is something she did to her throat when she tried to hang herself. *¿Quien sabe?* Who knows? She is old."

Lillian Monteverde arrived with two men, both gray, tall, and solemn. One wore the attire of a priest — a Franciscan; the other man's clothing was rumpled from travel. He kept his solemn expression when he knelt beside the pallet to examine the bandaging, which he said would have to be removed in order for him to see the extent of the injury.

There was not a sound in the hut, but beyond it life was being lived as it had for generations — dogs barked, children yelled, occasionally some distant cattle would bawl and, while concerned people came as far as the door to look in, none ventured to enter.

The medical man, old at his profession, showed nothing on his face as he examined the wound. He cleansed it with water, sprinkled some sharp-scented powder on it, told the *mayordomo* and the priest to hold Toby while ragged flesh was cut away and the wound was closed.

Toby fainted. Lillian Monteverde filled a cup with red wine and knelt, waiting for him to regain consciousness, which did not occur until the doctor was leaning back wiping his hands on a wet rag. Toby drank the wine feebly and smiled up at the stunning woman. He managed a quavery, *"Gracias."*

Juanita Flores pushed roughly through the watchers in the doorway and Salazar scowled at her. In Spanish he told her to wait outside; instead she sank to both knees beside the doctor, who faced her, saw *la patrona*'s faint nod, and spoke flawless Spanish when he said, "Look you, *señora*. . . ."

"¡Señorita!"

"Excuse me then . . . *señorita.* You see this blue bottle? Twice each day you remove the bandage, mix water with the contents of the blue bottle, wash the wound. Sprinkle some of this powder on it, then put on another bandage. Wash your hands often, please."

Juanita Flores's respect for the cloth extended to the priest, but not to *gringo* doctors who were rare. Her faith in those who cured people was only with *las curanderas,* the old women whose knowledge of herbal medicine was extensive, as were other practices with merit but which made trained physicians shudder. To prevent fever in open wounds, for example, a chicken was slain, split open, and put on the injury to suck away infection.

Juanita Flores did not question the doctor's ability, but she showed her lack of respect when she brashly said, "A tighter bandage would close the wound."

The doctor got stiffly to his feet and was rolling down a sleeve when he replied. "*Señorita,* I cannot sew the wound closed. There is much swelling. More swelling would tear away the stitches."

Juanita Flores smiled up at the doctor. "Not sew it, *señor,* pull it a little more closed with bandages each day."

The doctor rolled his eyes, jerked his head at Lillian Monteverde. When they were outside, he said, "Keep her away from your sister-in-law. As for him in there . . . well . . . let her practice her curing. It won't harm him."

The doctor and *la patrona* returned to the house, leaving the priest behind. He was a handsome man in his late fifties. He leaned to touch the shoulder of Juanita Flores and repeated to her in English: "Wash the wound often with the medicine from the blue bottle. Use the powder often. It will assure his recovery, if you wash your hands each time you work on him."

He did not see the testy fire in the woman's eyes because he straightened up to speak to Toby. They talked for a long time and might have spoken longer if Juanita Flores hadn't shown impatience with the long, rambling conversation, and the *mayordomo* seemed also to be getting impatient.

When the priest finally left, Juanita Flores rolled her eyes again and grumbled to Salazar, who nodded as she said, "They spend ten minutes at graveside pleading God's favor for a soul, but when this one talked to Toby, he asked questions I would have been embarrassed to ask of my own sister."

Salazar agreed, also in Spanish. "It is their trade, *chiquita.* They want to know all they can about people. Where Toby worked, who his friends had been, what pains he had suffered." Salazar sighed, went to the doorway, hesitated as he looked back, and said, "I am hungry."

Juanita Flores smiled. "Excitement to a man your age brings hunger. Return in half an hour."

Salazar glared. "That is the second time this day you have called me an old man. Let me say to you. . . ."

Toby interrupted to ask for more wine. After Juanita Flores refilled the tin cup and held it for him to drink, she looked over her shoulder. The *mayordomo* was gone.

She now knew what his particular irritant was and, knowing, in the future would avoid any reference to age. A successful huntress used the arrows of foresight.

Chapter Thirteen

Word From Trabajo

Tía Maria died in her sleep which, the priest solemnly told Lillian Monteverde, was God's way of taking the innocent and the deserving who were helpless.

He visited Toby one last time before he and the doctor saddled up for the long ride home.

They were alone. It was shortly before mid-morning when all but the young and the very old were busy tending the interests of Trinitaria.

It was cool in the hut. There were flies because the door hadn't been closed the night before. They did no more than scout up Toby; the odor of strong medicine sent them to the ragged, filthy, blood-soaked trousers and shirt left in a corner by Juanita Flores.

The priest pulled a bench to the side of the pallet, asked Toby if there was anything he wanted. Toby asked for a cup of red wine. As the holy father went to comply, he kept his back to Toby while liberally watering the wine. He poured a little wine into a cup for himself, returned to the stool, handed Toby a cup, and spoke in English.

"If what I have heard is true, then you killed two men who had to die." The priest faintly smiled. "It was God's will or it could not have happened . . . but . . . I think you should do something . . . learn to do something wise men of experience do."

Toby sipped wine as he said, "Father . . . ?"

"Toby, for everything that happens in life there is an aftermath. For every action there is a reaction. Do you understand?"

"No."

"You killed two men who worked for the state of Colorado. That was your objective and it was done. But those men were allied with the law. It is my guess Colorado will send someone to Trabajo to find you. Because what was done happened in New Mexico, Colorado will have to send lawmen authorized to operate anywhere. U.S. Marshals."

Toby put the cup aside still half full. "But, Father, there was two of 'em, an' I gave Bannion a chance, fair and square. That's what I'll tell the marshal, that's what folks in Trabajo will tell him."

The priest emptied his cup and held it loosely in one hand, dispassionately gazing at the wounded man. "Were you in prison up north?"

"Yes, almost two years."

"For stealing a horse?"

"Yes, but I didn't steal him, he was gave. . . ."

"Toby, consider this. If they want you, they will take you back with them. If something happens to you before they get back . . . well . . . you were sent to prison for horse stealing. They can make you out as bad as they wish. I won't say this will happen, but I've known of times when it did. Especially if there's a price on your head, or if you are troublesome on the ride back."

Toby propped himself up, and asked the priest why he was saying these things. The priest arose, put his cup on the table, and returned. He stood looking down as he replied. "The old woman died. That leaves her niece sad. She will continue to be sad for some time. Toby, if you are here when the marshal arrives . . . maybe more than one marshal . . . how will she react? It won't matter whether she tries to protect a Trinitaria rider or not. With Mexican law it could have been handled differently. She could buy your safety. With federal marshals, if she tries bribery to protect you. . . ."

"You want me to leave Trinitaria?"

"What you do is up to you. What I'm telling you is that these people are like a family, a clan; if one is in trouble, it becomes personal with all of them. What I'm saying is that if federal lawmen enter this yard, there's a very good chance the people of Trinitaria will resist if they try to take you away. You know what that means . . . killing. Right at this time in her life Lillian Monteverde does not need more grief." The priest paused. "I know you like it here, want to stay. I know you've never had a home or a family. Toby, the aftermath of those two killings . . . remember what I said, for everything that happens there is an aftermath. Now I have to go back to the house. I know it will hurt to leave."

The *mayordomo* walked in as studiously as an owl. He had been at the main house with *la patrona* helping to plan *Tía* Maria's burial.

He nodded to Toby, got himself a cup of red wine, and sank tiredly at the table. He asked how Toby felt without looking at the younger man. It was one of those perfunctory things a man was expected to say and it sounded that way. The only time the *mayordomo* looked at the younger man was when he asked why the priest had come.

Toby's answer was succinct. "He thinks federal marshals will come because Bannion and the other man were part of the law. He said the best thing for me to do is leave, otherwise *la patrona* . . . all of you will suffer."

Salazar snorted. "I think he is right about one thing. There will be someone come down here for the wagon, the team, and the bodies. For them they must arrive very soon because in Trabajo they will bury them without delay. If someone comes from up north . . . ," Salazar shrugged. "Let them do it."

Toby finished the watered wine and shifted under the blankets. Salazar spoke quickly. "Don't do that. It will start the bleeding." He made a death's head smile. "And did the priest say how you were to ride away . . . with a leg cut almost to the bone?" The *mayordomo* arose to depart. He used Spanish this time when he spoke. "Be tranquil, *compañero.* You cannot leave until your leg will stand it, and that will be a long while. Leave the rest to others. Now rest."

Toby lay back. Rest? How does a man rest when the choice is to leave what he had become part of or stay and bring trouble to others?

The doctor appeared in the doorway. Toby nodded at him. "Come in."

As the older man crossed to the table and sat, he said, "I've heard the story of the killings in that village several times. I know what the priest told you." The doctor leaned with clasped hands between both knees. "If you try to ride away, somewhere people will find you dead. You lost much blood. It's probably borderline . . . but you can't afford to lose any more."

Toby studied the medical practitioner. He had never before known a doctor, not even a *curandera.* "It ain't a choice at all," he said. "If lawmen don't come for a month, I can leave maybe; but if they come, I expect it won't be no month."

The doctor arose and spoke dryly. "A month may not

do it. That is a terrible wound. You will have a bad scar. Maybe, in later life you will develop a limp. There was a lot of nerve and muscle damage." He started to turn away as he said, "We should be on our way. The priest is talking to the *Señora* Monteverde." He made a wry smile. "Priests are long-winded."

Whether all the doctor had said could be true, and it probably was, his final remark was indeed true because what the priest had to say to *la patrona* could not be expressed quickly. For Lillian Monteverde, with her sister-in-law dead in a dark bedroom, what the priest told her about Toby, which he had gleaned from their long conversation, added to her burden, but she was adamant about one thing.

"No, father, he can't leave. Even if he was able, running would convince the law he was a murderer." She shrugged. "But in his condition he couldn't ride ten miles."

"More likely five," the priest said. "*Señora,* has he told you much of his life?"

"No, but occasionally he would say something. . . ."

"*Señora,* there is a Spanish saying that easily applies to this situation . . . *el corazón en lágrimas* . . . a heart in tears. What it means is that when painful things happen to people over which they have no control, the pain of those things settles in the heart."

Lillian Monteverde had heard the term, but had not understood it until the death of her husband. The way the priest explained it now in reference to Toby, she nodded. The holy man broadened his explanation, using Toby as his subject. "When he was young, he found an abused colt, hid it in a farmer's shed, and cared for it. Do you understand why a little boy would do that? Because he had found something that needed him, something he could love."

La patrona looked up. "He told me about the colt."

"Did he tell you it was something that desperately needed him, and that he desperately needed? He was left at a workhouse when he was young, abandoned. Do you see? The man he killed in Trabajo had beaten a child. The child died. To Toby that colt needed him. He was something Toby could care for. When the farmer shot the colt, there was nothing he could do. But from the man who beat that boy who died in prison, because Toby is now a man, he could exact vengeance, which is what he did. *Señora,* he has never had a home, never been among people like those at Trinitaria. If he has to leave. . . ."

"Another tear of the heart, Father?"

"Yes. Exactly."

The clearing of a throat in the doorway ended the discussion. The priest faced the doctor. "Right away. I'm sorry, but there was something I had to say. Excuse me, *Señora.*"

After the men from Mission Dolores departed, the yard was quiet. Most of the riders were out somewhere; desert ranches required a constant change of graze. Today the *mayordomo* was out with the others. They had successfully trailed those *orejano*-eyed longhorns to water days earlier, but there were two animals who cut back, the one-horned old razorback cow and her leggy, but undernourished, calf.

When she came into the yard, there was a quick council among the old men along with some of the women. It was decided to corral the cow and her calf, which would be easier than trying to drive her away on foot, but it could also be dangerous. To everyone's astonishment the slobbering cow allowed herself, followed by the calf, to be herded into a corral.

Someone pitched her a hefty flake of hay, which she immediately trampled over as she ate. The calf appeared either not too bright or diffident. It contented itself with lipping up the hay the cow had walked on and which under normal circumstances other cattle would not eat.

Juanita Flores came to squat beside Toby's pallet to feed him a beef tamale some older woman had prepared. Until Toby had eaten half the tamale, he did not realize how hungry he was.

Juanita Flores smiled broadly, heaved back upright, and went after more food. After Toby could eat no more, Juanita Flores said it was time to change the bandage. Toby was not entirely convinced this was so, but what could he say after she had brought him food?

Juanita talked incessantly, perhaps with some idea that he would be diverted; but she also did something much more likely to ease the pain. She soaked all the bandaging in water and did not remove anything until it was time, and then she continued to talk. Mostly it was a general discussion but, before she had finished re-bandaging the leg, Toby noticed her endless talk was focusing on the *mayordomo*.

She had no idea that the *gringo* had troubling thoughts of his own. It only occurred to her when *la patrona* appeared in the doorway as Juanita Flores was preparing to leave; then the barrel-built woman looked from one of them to the other, made the customary slight bowing of the head to *la patrona,* and left.

Toby not only needed an all-over bath, he also needed a shave. *La patrona*'s presence bothered him. If she noticed — and she probably did — there was no sign of it in her expression when she sat on a bench at the table and asked how his wound was healing and how he felt.

He said the leg did not hurt unless he moved and that, otherwise, excluding a constant thirst and hunger, he felt well enough. She held out a hand; when he did the same, she dropped a silver rosary onto his palm.

"*Tía* Maria's?" he asked.

"Yes."

Toby considered the worn beads and the face of the crucified one nearly obliterated by constant rubbing against someone. Lillian Monteverde said, "We will bury her tomorrow. We have our own graveyard. The men have already dug the grave."

Toby's eyes stung. "Is it far from here?"

She understood the question perfectly. "Too far, Toby. You are not to leave your bed . . . maybe in a month."

"*Señora, Tía* Maria needed love, and she gave love."

"You can't go, Toby. I know . . . she never let you out of her thoughts, and you handled it perfectly. I know she needed you. I understand all that was between the pair of you, but she wouldn't want you to risk re-opening the injury." *La patrona* smiled. "You need a shave."

He smiled back. He was self-conscious and embarrassed. "I can do that, nothing wrong with my hands. I'll borrow a razor."

The stunning woman arose. "I'll bring you one. It has ivory handles. It belonged to my husband." As she was about to leave, she also said, "I am very good at shaving men. I shaved my husband for more than a year before he died."

That evening when the riders returned a sweaty, dusty, and tired *mayordomo* came to Toby's *jacal*. He had seen the one-horned cow in the corral. As he sank down, he asked if Toby knew why the cow had been corralled.

Toby did not know she had been.

Because it was a minor thing and the *mayordomo* had other things on his mind, he did not mention the cow again. Instead, he gazed solemnly at the bandaged leg and shook his head.

Toby misjudged the headshake. "It's doing right well. Hardly no pain unless I move it."

The older man went to the jug, tipped red wine into a cup, and returned to the table, all without a word, but close association had given Toby an insight into how the older man functioned. He waited until Salazar was seated before saying. "You're plumb tuckered?"

Salazar considered the contents of his cup without seeming to have heard. He sipped, pushed the cup away, planted both arms atop the table, and gazed steadily at Toby.

"Three men came to Trabajo today. *Gringos.* Sanchez Ortiz came searching for Desdentado. He said the saloonman told Sanchez they were here because the prison wagon did not come back. One man is from the prison. He is to take the wagon back."

"And the other two are lawmen?"

"Yes. Do you want some wine?"

"Not right now."

The *mayordomo* arose. "I have to tell *la patrona.*"

Toby's dark, troubled mood returned. He was lying with both arms under his head, staring at the ceiling, when Manuel Acosta appeared in the doorway, wearing his wide, wet, toothless smile. He had a number of rawhide strips around one arm. His eyes were bright; his color was good.

He came to the side of the pallet and sat on the ground as he explained the purpose of his visit. "One time, when I was sick down in Mexico, an old man came to visit me every day. While I had to stay in bed, he taught me. Now watch. First, you learn braiding. A child can do this. Next he taught me how to make a square braid, then rawhide reins, and by the time I could leave the bed I could make a headstall, throat latch and all. Now you watch. Are you watching? Not with your eyes on the ceiling. Look, you!"

The thin, tall man's fingers were like spiders, constantly probing, twisting, interweaving. Desdentado was very adept. He had long fingers which helped. He worked fast, without speaking or looking up. When Juanita Flores came in, she stopped in her tracks until she understood, then scolded the toothless *vaquero* for encouraging Toby to sit up. Desdentado's retort was simple. "Only from the waist. He does not move the leg? You see?"

She nevertheless chased him away. Toby did not interfere although he had been intrigued by what the older man had been showing him. Braiding and plaiting were arts known in few places north of New Mexico territory. They would probably never have achieved popularity in *gringo* country anyway; the material used was rawhide, usually wet rawhide. Rawhide was untanned leather. Green hides attracted flies. Not just little flies, but some with startling blue rearends, which were as large as a thumbnail. Drew them by the hundreds.

An exasperated Juanita Flores rid the hut of flies by vigorously swinging an old towel and swearing in Spanish as she did so. When the last fly had fled out the door, she put both hands on her hips and said, "That Desdentado! All he does is make things of rawhide and drink red wine."

Toby offered a wan smile. "He needs a good woman, *señorita.*"

"Hah! He wouldn't know a good woman if he saw one.

Also, his house is filthy. What woman would want him." She straightened slowly, head cocked. Toby heard it too, the pealing of a little bell. Juanita Flores turned doorward swiftly. "*¡Cortejo funebre!*" she said, and fled from the house.

Toby saw people passing in sunshine beyond his doorway. He caught Manuel Acosta in the small crowd, who responded to his shout by coming as far as the door and peering warily inside. The barrel-shaped woman was gone, so Desdentado entered. Toby asked what was happening. Acosta replied solemnly. "They are going to bury *Tía* Maria. I have to go. I am one of the. . . ."

"Wait!"

Acosta stopped, looked down, and slowly shook his head. "No, *compañero.* There is no way to move you without starting the bleeding."

Acosta left. Toby sank back. The pealing little bell rang for some time before silence settled for about fifteen minutes, then someone with a powerful voice prayed over the grave in Spanish. Toby heard this without understanding one word in twenty.

His knowledge of funerals was limited but as the silence ran on he expected to hear singing. Not at *Tía* Maria's burial. There were mumbled prayers, many tears, much lamenting, but no singing. Finally, the man with the strong voice spoke again in Spanish. It had to be either a prayer or a eulogy. Toby groped for *Tía* Maria's rosary, gripped it tightly, and squeezed his eyes closed. Tears came anyway.

An hour later Juanita Flores returned. She was followed after an interval by the *mayordomo* who sat hat in hand as the woman brought them both a tin cup half full of red wine. Nobody spoke until later, when the *mayordomo* said, "When I was young, she was so beautiful.

She mothered all the children. Me, too." He sipped wine while Toby still gripped the rosary and Juanita Flores, for once, appreciated the need for silence.

Salazar finished his wine, smiled gently at Toby, and said, "I was surprised. For one so young . . . so ignorant . . . how you handled her. What you did for her was *grande.*" At Toby's blank look the *mayordomo* turned to Juanita Flores to supply the English word he had been unable to find.

She said, "Understanding with the heart."

Salazar nodded, and arose to leave. Juanita Flores spoke before he reached the door. "Where are you going? There is no work . . . today is for mourning."

He considered her from the doorway. "I'm going to see Desdentado. I think he hurt his wrist with the rope, lowering the box into the grave."

"You are going," she told him, "to drink wine with that old *boracho.* Stay here. I will make a meal."

He regarded her from the doorway as he quietly said, "I am going," and disappeared around the front of the *jacal.*

She turned toward Toby, but his eyes were tightly closed. There were tears. Juanita Flores left too, walking in the direction of her own hut. Not angry but very exasperated.

Chapter Fourteen

In the Name of the Law

The funeral took most of the day. Trinitaria had a small stone chapel erected under the exacting supervision of the long-dead first *patrón.*

Toby had seen the sturdy small building without his curiosity going any farther than to wonder why the stonework had been whitewashed. He had seen many granaries, but never before one painted white.

The yard was quiet; even the customary noise of children was muted. It was a day of mourning. For those such as the *mayordomo* who had known *Tía* Maria most of their lives, a single day of mourning was not enough; but after several days Trinitaria's normal activities were resumed. Among the older people prayers for *Tía* Maria were offered for years.

For Lillian Monteverde it was mandatory that she wear black for several months. When she visited Toby the fourth day after her sister-in-law's burial, it was a time of marveling; she looked more stunning. So much so that when she appeared in the hutment doorway, his breathing stopped for one long moment. But the beautiful woman had not come to be admired. As was her custom she was direct, almost brusque, when she told him she knew of the peace officers in Trabajo. It was her wish that, when they arrived in the yard, Toby should leave everything to her.

He didn't know what to say, she acted so formidable, so confident she could make U.S. Marshals go back to wherever they had come from simply because she wished them to. He eyed her with disbelief.

She said, "By now they have heard what happened in Trabajo many times. They will want your story, too. You tell them the truth." She abruptly changed the subject, making it seem more personal when she said, "I want you to stay."

He had no difficulty about that. "With this leg what else can I do?"

Her retort was less personal than direct. "What I meant was that they are not going to take you away." Her expression of defiance was clear. She added more by saying, "I won't allow you to be moved."

"*Señora,* if they have the authority, what can you do?"

"Toby, Trinitaria has had its own laws since before there was a United States."

He regarded her with bafflement. She was not making sense to Toby. The things she was intimating might have been true before Mexico had lost the territory to the United States long ago. However long Trinitaria had been in existence, regardless of having administered its own laws, as all the territory of New Mexico it was now part of the United States. All of its communities and people were subject to the laws of the United States.

She waited for him to speak; when he did not, she sank down on a bench at the table to speak again, but this time her voice was different. "Toby, I need you as much as I think you need Trinitaria."

He had a sudden recollection of the priest.

She continued speaking, more softly now in voice and

expression. "Trinitaria, I think, is the place you've been searching for; where you have loyal friends; where you will never be lonely nor feel unwanted . . . and I need someone I can understand, someone who knows what pain and loneliness are. Have you ever heard the saying 'tears of the heart?' "

"No, ma'am," he replied, completely in awe of the way her moods changed, as now when she was addressing him as a woman to a man, not as *la patrona* to a hired rider.

She hesitated, arose from the bench, and smiled at him. "Someday I'll explain. . . . You *will not* be taken from Trinitaria."

Once she departed, he continued to regard the doorway for a long time before sinking back on the pallet, troubled by something more than the arrival of the lawmen.

Juanita Flores appeared timidly in the doorway to ask if *la patrona* had gone. Toby nodded, and the heavy woman came as far as the table to say, "The *mayordomo* sent me to tell you Desdentado's nephew rode from Trabajo early to tell his uncle the *gringo* lawmen are coming. Two of them, one gray and heavy, the other much younger and, according to Desdentado's nephew, not a friendly man."

Toby asked where Salazar and the riders were. Juanita Flores answered candidly. "They were out looking for cattle to the east when this man from Trabajo met them. The *mayordomo* sent Ignacio to warn *la patrona,* then he and the others rode to find the pair of lawmen and follow them to the yard." Juanita Flores now asked a totally irrelevant question: "Are you hungry?"

Toby shook his head.

The woman regarded him for a moment before half filling a cup with red wine and handing it to him on her way out of the *jacal.* He sipped the wine. He had a strong respect for lawmen, if not for the law in particular — his being sentenced to prison by a rumpled, mean-eyed man up north on a charge that was not based on his testimony or the truth had provided all the skepticism he would need for the rest of his life. And there was the fact that the gunfight in Trabajo had been fair by every code he had ever heard of. The longer he lay there, staring at the ceiling, the more indignant he became over the power of the law — and lawmen — to ruin a man's life because of a callousness which seemed not to be interested in the truth.

He had no illusions about the law. Almost two years in the company of hardened criminals had convinced him that, in his present situation, nothing could stop them from taking him back with them if that was what they were coming to do. *La patrona* had sounded almost childlike when she had said she would not allow them to take Toby away with them. If she bullied them into riding away, when they returned they would have soldiers with them. Federal law could not be defied with impunity. Neither Toby nor anyone else had to be especially sagacious to know that.

The yard was quiet except for the challenging noise of that gaudy small rooster and a child crying somewhere as though its heart would break. It was hot, but dawns and dusks had been steadily becoming cooler as the summer wore along. In another few months the rains would come, if they came at all; but whether they did or not, nights would be cold and days crystal clear and cool, at times downright cold.

Juanita Flores came to wash, disinfect, and re-bandage the wound. She was usually quiet. Toby asked if the riders had come back yet. She shook her head as she told him not to move — please.

He waited until she was finished before also saying, "I owe you," and, from the bright look of her gaze, knew he should not have said that.

Three older men appeared as Juanita Flores was finishing. One of them, lined, dark and with eyes that missed nothing, said something to her in Spanish. She stood up, glaring, and replied in English. "You can't move him. The leg is healing well. Move him where?"

The older dark man answered in Spanish, which Toby had no difficulty understanding. "To the *hacienda.*"

Juanita Flores still stood defiantly but did not say a word. In fact she moved aside as the men approached the pallet, two at the head, one at the feet. She stopped them as they were bending. "Not like that, idiots. Put a board from his back down under the leg so it won't bend and start bleeding."

They straightened up, regarding her solemnly. One man left the hut and returned with a piece of old wood twelve inches wide. He and his companions raised Toby slightly, inserted the scantling, then took positions, and bent to lift.

Toby expected pain. They had a little difficulty getting him past the door but managed it and carried him in the direction of the main house with Juanita Flores watching from the *jacal* doorway. She turned aside only when the men had passed through the patio gateway beyond which she could not see.

She went to the hut of an old widow named Escobar, explained what had happened, and watched the old woman's face, wrinkled as a prune, break into a sly smile.

Juanita Flores said, "What is it, then?"

The old woman did not say what she thought, only what she had observed. What she thought was that age had advantages, one of which was a shrewd interpretation of things observed. What she said was, "If there is trouble coming, why then naturally *la patrona* wants the injured young man safely behind those very thick adobe walls." She smiled. No woman, not even the owner of a vast property like Trinitaria, goes so often to the *jacal* of a man injured, *gringo* or not, to look at a wound anyone could have told her was not going to kill him or he would already be dead.

The old woman asked about the *mayordomo* still wearing that infinitely wrinkled, wise smile. Juanita Flores gave an exasperated snort. "He is a stone. A man whose heart is dead to everything but Trinitaria."

"And Manuel Acosta?"

Juanita Flores was anything but dense. She stared at the old woman, "What about him?"

The old woman gathered her skirt close and sat on a bench. "He is a lonely man."

Juanita Flores arose. "Desdentado's *jacal* is filthy. Let me ask you . . . would it increase your heartbeat to look into the mouth of a grinning man who has no teeth?"

The old woman laughed behind her hand. She had few teeth herself. "No, I think not. But you are not getting younger. It is not God's will that single women of child-bearing age should not have a man."

Juanita Flores left the hut, heard something, and turned. Two riders were visible in the heat-wavery distance approaching the yard at a walk. Behind them, also riding at a walk, were the Trinitaria *vaqueros* being led by the *mayordomo*.

The pair of strangers had to know the *vaqueros* were no farther than a pistol shot behind them.

Juanita Flores poked her head in the old woman's hut and said, "Come look, *vieja*."

The old woman came, squinting her eyes nearly closed against the hot brilliance. She eventually said, "I have seen this before, back during the lifetime of *el patrón.*" She raised a claw-like hand to shield her gaze. "I can tell you this. Sometimes they do not ride back very far." The old woman ducked back into her hut.

The *vaqueros* turned off and loped around behind the barn. They were inside off-saddling when the pair of strangers appeared out front, dismounted, and tied their animals. The gray, heavier, older man came into the barn, approached Salazar and quietly said, "If you fellers figured on scarin' us, you didn't."

The riders stood like stone as the *mayordomo* said, "Mister, if we had wanted to scare you, we would have shot the horses out from under you."

The large man offered a wintry smile. "Where's the gent who owns this place? I'm U.S. Marshal Boyd Harding. The gent with me is a deputy U.S. marshal, Walt Rowe. The gent who owns this place . . . ?"

Salazar's dark eyes twinkled ironically. "Go to the main house. That is where the owner lives. We will care for your horses."

The large man nodded. "Much obliged. Do you folks speak English?"

"Not all," Salazar replied, and turned his back as he looped a latigo, ready to lift off the saddle.

The pair of large lawmen, one heavy, the other sinewy and lean with the movements of a panther, crossed to the wooden gate, shoved through, and the older man rattled the door with a gloved fist.

The young Indian woman who opened the door was smiling, but only for a moment. Facing her were two formidable-looking men, the kind she had seen often at trading posts and villages, men who rarely smiled and wore guns. Before she could speak a woman behind her standing in gloomy shade said, "What do you want?" and took the Indian's place in the doorway. Both lawmen looked steadily at her for a long moment before the older one produced a small steel circlet with black lettering inset on it. *La patrona* barely glanced at the badge as she repeated the question. "What do you want?"

The large, older man replied quietly, "We'd like to talk to your husband, ma'am."

"That's not possible. He has been dead seven years."

The older man's reply was in the same soft tone of voice. "I'm sorry to hear that."

Lillian Monteverde's expression did not change when she said, "What do you want?"

The younger man's face showed hostility at her attitude, but the large older man's bearing did not change as he withdrew a limp paper from a pocket and offered it to her. She did not even look at the extended hand. "Tell me, Marshal, for the last time . . . *what do you want?*"

The large man's face was expressionless as he pocketed the paper. His gaze, though, hardened when he answered. "We want to talk to a rider of yours named Toby Lincoln."

"What about?"

This time the lean, younger man answered. "About two killings in that village east of here, an' lady, you ain't makin' this any easier."

The large man cleared his throat. It sounded more like a growl. The younger man did not speak again.

The gray, older man still spoke softly but his eyes showed less amiability than before. "Ma'am, this rider of yours killed two men in the employ of the state of Colorado. That paper I showed you was an order of extradition from the New Mexican authorities allowing us to take this gunman back to Colorado to stand trial."

"On what charge, Marshal?"

"Murder. Ma'am, may we set down? It's hot an' my legs aren't what they used to be."

She closed the door at her back and gestured toward benches. The older man sat, but the hostile one remained standing. So did Lillian Monteverde.

She asked what the date was on the extradition order and, when the older man told her, she said, "That was before you could have known anything about the gunfight. And it wasn't murder."

The older lawman was briefly silent. He had been following his trade twenty-three years in which time he had met all kinds. The beautiful widow was defiant — well, hell, they all were. And Boyd Harding was well past fifty. In that length of time a man of his disposition learns many things, one of which is the obligation of his duty, but another thing was patience. It also helped that after many days in the saddle he was tired all the way through.

"Ma'am," he said quietly with considerable forbearance, "it came to the attention of the authorities in Colorado that the two men who come down here with a prison wagon an' extradition papers signed by the New Mexico territorial governor, to take back two outlaws bein' held here as thieves and who also had long records in Colorado, got shot in the performance of their duties. I was given the papers entitling me to take the feller who killed 'em back up north for trial."

Lillian Monteverde was a good listener — she had learned to be from her late husband. She said, "Marshal . . . ?"

"Harding, ma'am. Boyd Harding. This here is a deputy U.S. marshal. His name is Walt Rowe."

"Mister Harding, will you tell me how that extradition

order happens to say 'murder?' "

"Yes'm. That's what the superintendent of the prison wrote on it."

"Before he knew the facts, Mister Harding?"

"Ma'am, all I can tell you is that's what he wrote."

"And you read that . . . and came down here to arrest a murderer?"

"Yes'm."

"How many days did you spend in Trabajo?"

"We got here four days ago."

"Then you talked to people. Did they tell you it was murder?"

"Mostly, they said it was a fair fight. But we talked to a couple of fellers who said they saw a tall, skinny Trinitaria rider at the edge of the jailhouse behind the fellers who got shot. They said they was pretty sure when the firin' started, the feller who was behind the dead men shot the wagon driver from behind."

Lillian Monteverde was nonplused but rallied quickly. "These men who said the driver was shot from behind . . . can you tell me their names?"

The large man smiled. "No, ma'am. An' I'd take it kindly if you'd tell us where this Toby Lincoln is." He stood up, having said just about all he intended to say for the time being. "Ma'am, do you know where this man is?"

"Yes."

"Do you know that hidin' a wanted man can get you charged as an accessory?"

Lillian Monteverde's attitude changed. She said, "Marshal, you will be guests of Trinitaria overnight. I'll have the *mayordomo* show you to a vacant *jacal.*" She moved to the gate, reached through some overgrown flowering bushes, and rang a small bronze bell.

Salazar heard it, came briskly across the yard followed by Desdentado who showed none of his customary smile. The little bell was not rung often. When the two men reached the gate, Lillian Monteverde opened it as she said, "Marshal, this is *Señor* Salazar, the *mayordomo* . . . the foreman. He will see that you are settled. We will talk again in the morning."

Harding stopped the woman's brisk stride across the patio to the doorway. "Lady, we're right grateful for your hospitality, but I want to talk to Toby Lincoln."

"In the morning, Marshal."

As the pair of federal officers were following the *mayordomo,* Walt Rowe leaned and softly said, "He's here."

Harding nodded. "He was shot bad, Walt. Bad hurt men can't run."

Salazar showed them to a long-vacant hutment which was cobwebby and thick with dust. He pointed to an ancient pallet. "If you don't move much, both of you can sleep there." He turned to depart when the large older man said, "Mister, I got a question. Do you know where Toby Lincoln is?"

The *mayordomo* hesitated in the doorway long enough to say, "*¿Quien sabe?*" and left.

Walt Rowe looked around. "I'd as leave sleep outside."

Boyd Harding kicked the pallet; dust flew. "I've slept in worse," he said. "Fetch in the saddlebags. I never like goin' to bed hungry."

When the deputy marshal returned and dumped the saddlebags atop a rickety table, he said, "Boyd, that's some woman."

The older man sat down to yank off his boots. Lately his feet had taken to swelling in hot weather. "I'll tell you one thing, Walt. If Lincoln's bad hurt, she isn't goin' to let us take him, an' I'd say from the looks of those riders of hers that shagged us to the yard, if she says we don't take him an' we try anyway, someone's goin' to get hurt. Us. There should be four tins of sardines in my saddlebags. Two each."

Juanita Flores appeared in the doorway with two wooden platters of food. The lawmen looked around, not as surprised as they were grateful.

Juanita Flores crossed to the table, put the wooden trays on it, considered the *gringos,* smiled, and asked if they spoke Spanish. When they both shook their heads, her smile widened as she said in Spanish, "May you both die a miserable death."

The youngest lawman smiled back as he said, "Thanks, ma'am. I'm sure it's as good as you say it is."

Juanita Flores went outside, got no more than ten yards when she doubled over with laughter.

When she reached the *mayordomo*'s hut, he was sitting at the table, smoking a brown-paper *cigarillo.* He asked her what the *gringos* had said. When she told him what she had told them and what the youngest one had replied, the *mayordomo* broadly smiled.

She brought him a tin cup of watered red wine which he savored as he thought out loud. "They will want to take him away with them."

Juanita Flores whirled from the corner stove. "He can't travel, *jefe.*"

Salazar sounded irritated when he replied, "I know that. Do you think I came down in the last rain?"

"No," she shot back. "The rain before that."

He scarcely heard. "I don't like the idea of trouble with *norteamericano* law."

She was busy making supper and did not look around, but she had a comment to make. *"En el pais de las ciegos el tuerto será rey.*"

Salazar scowled at her back. "What are you talking about, woman?"

She turned to explain it in English. "In the land of the blind the one-eyed will be king. *Norteamericano* law is king. If *la patrona* defies it . . . this time the Monteverdes will regret it . . . very much."

The *mayordomo* finished his smoke, sipped from the tin cup, and regarded her back for a long time before arising to go outside where dusk and coolness had settled. It was inconceivable that a female, a woman, should have such perception. He waved over where Desdentado was sitting outside with a cup in his hand. Acosta waved back. Juanita Flores appeared in the doorway. "It is ready but, if you want to stand out there communing with the stars, I can keep it warm . . . *viejo.*"

He turned on her. She hadn't called him an old man for some time. The look on his face when he entered the house was enough. She would never do that again; but, of course, she had promised herself this same thing another time before.

The evening lingered; stars were everywhere above; there was not a breath of cooling air, and would not be until about midnight.

The *mayordomo* sat outside with Juanita Flores. She rolled and lighted a cigarette for him. He watched and was impressed at her dexterity. He had not spoken through supper. He also understood why she had made him the smoke. He smiled at her and would have spoken, but she raised a hand. "Excuse me. I will never use that word to you again. Besides, you are not old. Maybe in years . . . otherwise you are the match of any of them."

He did something he occasionally did with children,

but not too often. He put his arm around her shoulders. Neither of them moved until he had to lean to stamp out the smoke. By then the first little cooling breeze had arrived.

Chapter Fifteen

A Very Long Day

Toby had always been a good listener, as he now was when Lillian Monteverde told him of her meeting with the pair of federal lawmen.

He would have interrupted to protest, but he had learned at Trinitaria it was considered rude to do that. He waited until she had finished before saying, "Shot in the back? Ask Salazar, ask Manuel Acosta. Ask any of the folks in Trabajo who saw the fight! Shot in the back? By me? How could I have done it when I was facing them?"

La patrona wanly smiled. "In the morning I will send someone to Trabajo to find the men who said that. Toby, we have known each other a long time, since before you were shot; I could swear by the Holy Cross you wouldn't shoot a man in the back . . . but . . . that's why the marshals rode here. What must be done is prove it did not happen like that. For that I'll send the *mayordomo* and Desdentado to Trabajo to find the ones who said that. Don't be upset."

He glared at her. "Upset? Someone says you're a back-shooter an'. . . ."

"Toby, listen to me . . . you can't even stand up. I can. And I've fought these little private wars many times. Don't worry."

La patrona sent the smiling young Indian woman to bathe him. He recoiled from that with an anxiety equivalent to his agitation over the charge that he had shot one of his victims in the back. The Indian retreated, told *la patrona* he would not allow her to touch him. Lillian Monteverde smiled, sent the Indian woman to a very old and gloomy *jacal* on the outskirts for a woman to bathe Toby.

When she arrived, ancient beyond recall, withered, lined and nearly toothless, she entered Toby's room, smiled once, then began arranging towels, soap, and a basin of warm water. As she turned to roll up her sleeves, she said, "*¿Habla español?*"

He shook his head, eyeing the old woman warily.

She paused a long moment, clearly ordering her thoughts in another language before speaking. "You will to me listen, please. My name is Emilia Escobar. Forty years ago my husband was *mayordomo*. I am being understood, Mister?"

"*Si.* Yes."

"Prepare yourself then for an all-over bath." When she said that, the old woman rolled up both sleeves, soaked a cloth in the basin, took a bar of brown soap, and approached the bed. She lowered the covers to Toby's middle, smiled, and went to work. Her claw-like hands were surprisingly strong as were her withered arms. She scrubbed, rinsed, and re-scrubbed. She said nothing. Her face showed clear concentration on what she was doing.

Toby reddened as she impersonally kept scrubbing, even after she had eased him up on his uninjured leg and scrubbed even harder. She got the bedding thoroughly soaked and did not stop until he was rosy-pink and again on his back. Then she smiled. "The bandage belongs to Juanita Flores. I won't touch it." She sat down, regarding him from shrew-like, bright, very dark eyes. "Do you know Desdentado?" she asked.

Toby nodded.

"He told me about the fight in Trabajo. To Trabajo I have not been since my husband died. Mister," she said, arising and beginning to gather the bathing articles with her back to Toby, "you must not worry. *La patrona* knows about these things." She turned the bright gaze back on Toby. "There is a good woman. Do you hear me?"

He nodded again, "*Si, Señora.*"

She smiled. "*El mayordomo.* Juanita Flores you know too?"

"*Si.* Yes."

"Juanita Flores is a single woman. The *mayordomo* is in need of a good woman. You are his *compañero.* Could you then tell him he needs Juanita Flores?"

Before Toby could reply a firm voice from the doorway said something in Spanish. Emilia Escobar quickly gathered her things and left the room. Lillian Monteverde entered, carrying a lamp which had been turned up to its maximum. It brightened everything, from the walls, the Spartan furnishing, to the man in the bed who badly needed a shave. She sat on a chair and considered Toby. During the silence between them he could not find a flaw. Even the pigeon-wings of silver at her temples made a perfect contrast with her otherwise very black hair.

She said, "Juanita wants to change the bandage. I told her in the morning. Toby, do you know what will happen if those law men try to take you away?"

"I expect the wound will bust open."

She nodded about that, but it was not what she had meant, so she explained. "Yes. All the healing would be undone. The doctor said you could not lose more blood.

Toby, I have eight *vaqueros.* They have accepted you. They consider you as much a part of Trinitaria as they are. They will not allow these *gringos* to take you away."

He blew out a silent long breath.

She continued. "I know how you were sent to prison, and that over a horse. Do you know what *gringo* law will do to you for shooting two men?"

"It was a fair fight, ma'am."

"Yes, I know that. I talked to Desdentado and the *mayordomo.* They will go to the village first thing in the morning to find the men who said you shot one of those men in the back." She leaned forward a little. "In the morning I'll bring those marshals in here. I want them to talk to you, to others, to me, until Manuel Acosta and the *mayordomo* return. Do you understand?"

"Yes'm. You want to keep them lawmen here as long as you can."

She smiled and arose. "Talk, Toby. Talk their legs off. *Buenos noches.*"

He did not sleep well until about dawn; then he slept so soundly that when the Indian woman brought breakfast he was still sleeping.

What eventually awakened him were voices in the parlor. Two men and a woman were talking. He sat up, rubbed his eyes, felt the beard stubble, propped himself up, and waited. Two things occurred almost simultaneously: Juanita Flores arrived with the bottles and bandaging and *la patrona* appeared in the doorway with two strangers, one big and gray, the other slimmer, wearing an expression of masked hostility. Juanita Flores fled, leaving behind her bottles and bandaging cloth.

The big hulk of an older man approached the bed, gazed a moment at Toby, then extended a ham-sized hand. "U.S. Marshal Boyd Harding, Mister Lincoln." The gorilla-built older man sat down, making a small smile. "No kin to old Abe, by any chance?"

Toby had heard similar remarks many times. He did not smile as he said, "No sir."

The deputy marshal remained standing, not once taking his eyes off the man in the bed, nor did he nod or extend a hand when Marshal Harding introduced them.

The marshal cleared his throat. "Mind showin' us your wound, Mister Lincoln?"

Before Toby could raise up and lean to lower the blankets, Lillian Monteverde appeared. She had been standing against the wall outside. She lowered the blankets, wearing a flinty expression.

Both men edged closer and leaned. Marshal Harding pursed his lips but his deputy said, "Don't mean nothing, Boyd. I've seen 'em wearin' them thick bandages before with nothin' under 'em."

Marshal Harding raised his steely gaze to *la patrona* who ignored him to glare at Walt Rowe. The deputy made a bleak smile. "Lady, you want to unwrap it, or shall we?"

Lillian leaned, studied the bandage, found where it had been tied, gently released the knot and even more tenderly began the unwinding process. She did not expose the entire wound because the older man raised a hand. Toby's leg was still discolored above and below the bandaging. He said, "Wrap it back up, ma'am," and turned to his deputy with an expression of annoyance but he said nothing. Deputy Marshal Rowe moved away, found a bench, and sank down on it.

The large man had a question for Toby. "How'd the fight start, Mister Lincoln?"

"When I heard Bannion would be on the prison wagon,

I waited because I had a score to settle with him."

"From somethin' he did while you was in prison?"

"There was a boy named Abel, sickly, runty. Helpless, Marshal. When he got too bad off to work, Bannion come to our cell and hit him hard with a club. Abel died."

Harding said, "I see. You wanted to settle for this boy?"

"Yes sir."

"An' the other one, the feller drivin' the prison wagon . . . did you want him too?"

"No. Never seen him before in my life."

"Was he facing you when you shot him?"

"Yes sir. He was wearing one of those double-action pistols."

"An' he went for it an' you shot him?"

"Well," Toby replied, and looked past at the hostile deputy marshal and back, "what happened was . . . I aimed at Bannion. I hit that other feller instead."

The deputy snorted. Marshal Harding acted as though he had heard nothing. "Mister Lincoln, we got reason to believe the wagon driver was shot from behind."

Toby riveted the older man with a stare. "No sir. I was tryin' to hit Bannion. The bullet hit the other feller in the chest. That's exactly how it happened. There was no one behind the wagon driver."

Marshal Harding leaned back in the chair, ranged a look around the room, let it linger briefly on the handsome, very erect, clearly hostile woman across the bed from him, then sighed and said, "I got a murder warrant for your arrest, Mister Lincoln, an' extradition papers allowin' me to take you back to Colorado to stand trial." He paused before also saying, "Ma'am, you got a Mexican rider. I forget his name, but he's got no teeth."

From his chair the deputy marshal said, "Manuel Acosta!"

For the second time he was ignored by the older man. "Ma'am . . . ?"

"Yes, there is a *vaquero* named Manuel Acosta. He has no teeth. He is called Desdentado, which means the toothless one."

"I'd like to talk to him. He's a feller we was told was behind the wagon driver."

"And you think he killed this wagon driver?"

"I don't know. We was told it was Lincoln did both killings, but we was also told the wagon driver was shot in the back up high, not from in front. That's why I'd like to talk to Acosta . . . or whatever you call him. I'd like him to tell me exactly where he was standin' when the shootin' started. Is he handy, ma'am?"

"No. If you had told me last night you wanted him, I would have kept him here. No, he is not here."

"But he'll be back?"

"Yes, when the riders return. Marshal, Trinitaria is a large holding. We run about eight hundred cows, counting bulls, steers which are altered in the spring before fly time, and heifers. I need a large crew. Those men who trailed you yesterday were Trinitaria riders."

Marshal Harding listened to everything *la patrona* said then arose to ask another question. "When will your riders come in, ma'am?"

"Usually a little before supper time. Marshal, if you wish, I'll send Manuel Acosta to your *jacal* as soon as he returns. The *mayordomo* was also in Trabajo during the gun fight."

Harding nodded. "An' he'll be out with your riders, too?"

Lillian Monteverde lied with a clear conscience. "Yes.

I will send them both to you. Marshal, it is now the hottest time of the day. I'll have refreshments sent to your *jacal.* It is our custom to sleep through the worst hours of heat. You could do the same since the riders you want won't return to the yard until supper time."

As the large man stood regarding her, interested in how cooperative she was today as opposed to her clear hostility yesterday, she asked him a question. "You have a warrant for Toby Lincoln?"

He inclined his head without taking his eyes off her. Marshal Harding was seasoned and experienced. He waited for her next remark.

Lillian Monteverde did not keep him waiting. She said, "Do you need another warrant if you can prove one of my riders shot the wagon driver?"

"Not exactly, ma'am. We got the warrant for Lincoln. We're supposed to fetch him back up north to be tried. But you're wonderin', do we have a warrant for this Acosta feller. No ma'am, we don't have. But we're federal officers. We got authority to operate anywhere within the United States an' that includes New Mexico territory. If we find sound reason to take this Acosta into custody on suspicion of murder, we can do it under the law. But we'd have to deliver him to the nearest New Mexico authorities."

"You couldn't take him to Colorado?"

Harding was tiring of this, so he was a little sharp when he said, "Lady, if Acosta back-shot a man in New Mexico, why would we take him to Colorado where he *didn't* shoot the feller in the back?"

Lillian Monteverde lowered her eyes, then raised them as she said, "Excuse me. I don't know United States law. I'll have a meal sent to your *jacal.*"

She was the last to pass beyond the doorway. She hesitated, looked back, and winked at Toby.

Juanita Flores returned. She was sweating. It was fiercely hot wherever a person was exposed and she had crossed the full length of the yard from the Escobar *jacal.*

She was business-like, clucked a little over finding the bandage had been tampered with, and raised black eyes to Toby's face. "They didn't believe you got shot?"

He nodded without commenting. His thoughts were on the meeting with the marshals. It had not seemed to him that Lillian Monteverde had anything to wink about at the doorway. According to his lights she hadn't won any arguments. He only brightened when he recalled her hospitable offer to send a meal to the lawmen's little house and the marshal's apparent gratitude for her solicitude. *That* would delay things.

He winced and Juanita Flores apologized before looking up as she said, "You heal very fast." She held up a stiff forefinger. "That's how the scar will look. That deep and that wide." Juanita Flores disinfected from the blue bottle and sprinkled powder. Toby said, "Not so much . . . please."

She leaned back, surprised. "You want to save it for another time?"

"No. I want to save it for that crazy cow in the corral. Get rid of her maggots."

Juanita Flores departed with her medicine and bandaging cloth. She met Lillian Monteverde in the parlor and was asked how the wound was healing.

She blurted out, "Do you know what he said? To save some medicine for that one-horned cow in the corral, the one that would have killed *Tía* Maria and the *mayordomo.*"

La patrona smiled slightly. "But how is the wound?"

"It will have a scar," she replied, holding up on a rigid

finger. "About that size and maybe that deep. Is it healing very well? The *gringo* is healthy."

They left Toby alone until shortly before supper time, then Lillian Monteverde appeared with a basin, a towel, and a folded straight razor with ivory handles.

Toby watched her handle the razor, which she did deftly, but that was still a formidable length of very sharp steel. He said, "A beard would make me more . . . *macho?*"

She laughed. He had never heard her laugh before. "You don't need hair on your face to be a man. You *are* a man." She mixed a heavy froth in an old shaving mug, leaned and, when he would have spoken, she accidentally swept the shaving brush across his mouth.

He remained as still as a stone during the process of shaving. While the razor was sharp, his beard had been growing since he'd been wounded. Getting a smooth face was, in a manner, torture.

When she finished and washed off the soap, she stood back and said, "You look like . . . you should shave often."

She gathered her shaving things and hesitated before departing to add: "They were fed well. They will rest until sundown. Laudanum makes people drowsy even if they don't have full stomachs."

"Laudanum, ma'am?"

"It is something when put in wine makes people sleep."

He stopped her before she reached the door. "I never had folks take me in like you've done. I owe you, Miz Monteverde."

She departed without speaking which left Toby wondering if he had offended her by using her name. Everyone else referred to Lillian Monteverde as *la patrona.* He would remember not to make that mistake again.

He slept through the shimmering hours of the day, cool and comfortable in a bedroom with sparse but impressive furniture, protected from the heat by walls of mud, manure, and straw which were three feet thick.

Something awakened him. The ancient Escobar woman was watching him from the doorway. The house was totally quiet. So was the yard, but he did not know that. The old woman moved soundlessly into the room and sat at his bedside. She smiled and said, "You had kindness for *Tía* Maria. In this place even the walls have eyes. God will remember that kindness of a certainty. My own husband liked *gringos.* Many people don't. He was a wise man. To him all men were the same, with red blood and two eyes and two ears. Some he said were better than others, but that had nothing to do with brown hides or white hides. He taught me English which I speak well, eh?"

Toby liked Emilia Escobar. As he visited with her in the deathly quiet house, he thought she probably knew more secrets about Trinitaria than anyone alive, and he was right. What he did not know was that, while her body was nearing the end of its usefulness, her mind was still as sharp as a dagger.

She arose to depart. "I am not supposed to be here, but the others are all at siesta." She patted his hand and said, "Do not leave. Ever. Trust in God. He knows you better than anyone. *Adios, compañero.*"

Chapter Sixteen

The Unexpected

Toby grimaced after the old woman. Leave? He wasn't going to leave for a long time, not because he did not think that departing would resolve the trouble with the federal lawmen, but simply because he could not get out of bed and put weight on his wounded leg. During the healing process the leg had lost muscular strength. Even when he raised it beneath the covers, it responded with wobbly uncertainty.

By mid-morning when the federal marshals came to see him again he was beginning to feel resigned. He wanted to talk to the *mayordomo;* instead he got Marshal Harding, and Deputy Marshal Walt Rowe who for once did not glare. This morning Rowe's expression was one of puzzlement. He sat on the same distant chair he'd used the day before while the moose of a man took the chair closest to the bed. Harding considered Toby for a moment before speaking.

"That's a good shave you got, Mister Lincoln." That was the marshal's customary method for opening conversations — with words designed to put at ease whomever he was talking to. It worked with Toby as it had with hundreds of others in different places.

"It itched, Marshal. I never tried to grow whiskers." Toby allowed the pleasantries to end, watched the large man, and waited.

"Mister Lincoln, odd thing happened yesterday evening. When me'n Mister Rowe was cleanin' up, an old Mexican, gray as a badger, and another Mexican . . . without no teeth . . . come to our *jacal.*"

Toby nodded. That would be Desdentado and the *mayordomo.*

The large man continued speaking in an unhurried, steady voice. "Do you know many New Mexicans in the area, Mister Lincoln?"

"Well, the riders on Trinitaria, maybe a few folks in the village. One of 'em's a black man. He's got a sort of tradin' and livery business."

"Do you know a man named Arturo Iturbide an' one named Juan Sisco?"

Toby thought briefly before shaking his head. "Don't believe I do. Why?"

The big man leaned back to get more comfortable while speaking. "Them gents who come to our hut last evenin' had them other two with them. You don't know them?"

"Sisco and Iturbide? No, never heard of 'em, Marshal."

"Well, they're the fellers who dug the graves for Bannion and the wagon driver. They're the fellers in Trabajo who told us the wagon driver was shot from behind. They said the bullet hit him in the back, high up, and come out in front."

Toby was gaining color in his face even before the large man had finished his recital. "They're lyin' sons-of-bitches. I already told you how the wagon man got hit; the slug went wide when I shot at Bannion."

Harding was impassive. "Maybe. The feller with no teeth told us you was fast drawin' but an awful shot at hittin'. He told us he sort of coached you. The other feller said he was in a doorway an' could see everythin' as it happened an' no one was behind the wagon driver."

Toby nodded slightly. "It's up to you, ain't it? Either I back-shot the scrawny feller, or I didn't. The gospel truth is I didn't."

"Well, no, Mister Lincoln, it's not up to me. It's up to whatever judge you get up in Colorado. Walt an' I'll tell exactly what we heard down here. . . ."

"How can you try me in Colorado for somethin' that happened in New Mexico territory?"

"If we was sheriffs or constables, somethin' like that, we couldn't. But we're federal lawmen. There's a federal court up in the Denver settlement in Colorado. There's no federal court down here. You understand?"

Toby understood what Marshal Harding had explained, but he did not understand being tried in a court so distant from where the shooting had occurred, among people who knew nothing of the fight. He had a question for the big lawman.

"Do you believe a person could be sent to prison for not stealing a horse, but because strangers said he did steal it?"

Marshal Harding sat a moment sorting that out. Eventually he said, "You're sayin' you didn't steal a horse?"

"That's gospel truth, Marshal. I didn't steal the horse . . . but I spent almost two years in prison because the judge hated horse thieves."

Deputy Walt Rowe spoke harshly from the far side of the room. "We heard about you'n that horse. Some cowman gave it to you." Rowe snorted derisively. "Cowmen just naturally give sixty-dollar workin' stock horses to kids usin' cotton rope to hold up their britches and strings tyin' their shoes."

Toby looked steadily past the large man to meet the sneer on the deputy's face. "I wish I could get out of this bed," he said. "You pig-headed son-of-a-bitch."

Deputy Rowe came out of his chair in one lithe movement. He stood poised for a long moment, then relaxed. "I wish you could get out of that bed too," he said, and sat back down.

Marshal Harding had watched Toby throughout the flare-up. When it was finished, he said, "They tell me there's a place called Mission Dolores about sixty miles from here, where they got a telegraph."

Toby nodded without speaking. He was still fired up.

Marshal Harding arose with a sigh. A sixty-mile ride with the heat bad enough to fry dough-cakes on a rock was nothing he looked forward to. He gazed dispassionately at Toby, then spoke again. "We'll haul you back in the prison wagon. Get some hay or blankets." He turned and jerked his head. Walt Rowe arose to follow the large man out of the room without once looking at Toby.

When Lillian Monteverde arrived an hour or so later, she had the *mayordomo* with her. Marshal Harding had told *la patrona* he had to find a telegraph so he could explain what had happened on the south desert. She was coolly solicitous, offering to send one of her *vaqueros* to the Mission Dolores settlement if the lawman would print the message he wanted transmitted northward. Harding might have accepted the offer but his deputy thanked *la patrona* coldly and told her U.S. Marshals did not need others to do their work for them.

While she was explaining this to Toby, the *mayordomo* stood back a few steps, nodding his head. Toby was less interested in *la patrona*'s offer than he was in the men who had been brought from Trabajo by Desdentado and Salazar: Iturbide and Sisco. He asked Salazar about them. The *mayordomo* spread his hands palms down in a deprecating way.

"Drunks," he said. "Petty thieves, worthless animals who lie when the truth would be simpler. On the ride back Desdentado and I talked to them. They said the thin man had two bullet holes, one in front, another in back. They told us they knew if they said something like that those *gringo* lawmen might pay them. So they said it . . . and the young law officer gave them each a silver dollar."

"Where are Sisco and Iturbide now?" Toby asked.

Salazar showed a faint, bitter smile. "We took them to see the *gringos.* They told their story, said they had lied because it might bring them some money. They showed the big *gringo* the silver dollars his deputy had given them. The big man told me to tie them up somewhere. He would talk to them again."

Lillian Monteverde had stood silently during this exchange, but when it was finished she addressed Toby. "They want to put straw in the prison wagon and take you up north in it."

Toby would have spoken, but the *mayordomo* excused himself and left. Before Toby could speak the next time *la patrona* beat him to it.

"It is not going to happen. Even if you were healed, they would not take you north with them."

He smiled a trifle ruefully at her. "Lady, you get a U.S. Marshal hurt an' the next fellers to ride into the yard will be the Army."

She smiled enigmatically, said, "We'll see," and left the room.

Toby cursed under his breath. He had learned in prison

how to swear a full sixty seconds without repeating himself.

He tried moving the leg, felt wetness inside the bandage, and swore again. He leaned to pull a chair close and muscled his upper body while keeping the injured leg straight, and got into a chair.

Then what? he asked himself, put his face in both hands, and was sitting like that when Juanita Flores came through the doorway and stopped with a sharp intake of breath. She turned and fled through the house until she found *la patrona.* In frantic Spanish, running the words together, she told Lillian Monteverde that Toby was out of the bed.

It took three women to lift him back into the bed, Juanita Flores, Lillian Monteverde, and the pleasant-tempered Indian.

La patrona dismissed the others, pulled the chair close, and used a small lace handkerchief to wipe mingled sweat and tears of frustration off his face. He kept his eyes squeezed closed. She took one of his hands and held it.

"Toby, listen to me. You will be all right. I asked you to believe in me. Do it! They will not take you away."

He spoke harshly to her. "What can you do? *Gringo* law does what it wants to do."

"No! Not on. . . ."

"Gawddammit, you don't understand. They'll haul me out of here if they got to kill every man you got."

She squeezed his hand, hard. "Toby, Trinitaria has met Apaches, *bandoleros* up out of Mexico, *gringo* renegades, even soldiers left over from the Civil War. We are still here, the others are not. Toby. . . ."

He swung his face toward her; she was leaning close. For two seconds she did not pull back, but eventually she did as he spoke.

"What I did, Bannion had comin', but that was supposed to settle it. Now I got you and other folks tangled up in my mess. I wish now I'd just beat that son-of-a-bitch with my hands."

She leaned to say, "It doesn't matter now what you should have done. . . ."

"I know that, dammit." He looked steadily at her from a distance of less than eighteen inches. "Help me."

"I *am* helping you."

"No! Loan me one of your light buggies an' a good horse."

She put two cool fingers across his lips. "I won't do that and, if I did, you wouldn't go two miles. You'd faint and bleed to death. Toby! Be sensible!"

He was perspiring, and it wasn't hot in the room. She was as tense as a coiled spring. They regarded each other for a long moment before he spoke again, most of the wild exasperation gone from his voice.

"Give me one reason, ma'am, for you to do this for me. I got nothin' an' came from nowhere. I can't even read very good." His voice was rising when he said the rest of it. "You fight the law, the Army, an' you'll get burnt to the ground, your folks will get shot or drove off with whips, an' you. . . ."

What she did couldn't have stunned him more if she poured a bucket of cold water over his head. She leaned forward and kissed him squarely on the mouth!

For ten seconds afterwards when she leaned away, he stared without blinking, then Lillian Monteverde arose and went quickly out of the room. In the kitchen she startled the Indian woman. "Draw a bath for me. Cold water from the pump. Do it now!"

More than an hour later the Indian woman came to say that the large man was at the front door. Lillian told the woman to take him some cold water and ask him to be comfortable on the patio; she would come as soon as she could.

It was good that Marshal Harding was a patient man. He sat in shade made fragrant from flowers, sipped the water, shoved out his legs to relax while his thoughts wandered from what he had come to say, to the other complications of his mission. He heard two men calling back and forth in Spanish, thought it was an interesting language. When Lillian Monteverde appeared, face slightly flushed but with her dark eyes as unyielding as ever, he arose to say, "I don't want the blame for moving Toby Lincoln in the prison wagon if he starts bleeding. I sent Walt Rowe to Mission Dolores to telegraph up north explaining what could happen if he's moved. If you don't mind, I'd like to stay here until Walt gets back. I know, Lincoln can't run off, but all the same. . . ."

She smiled at the large man, sat opposite his bench, and spoke in a pleasant voice. "I am glad you don't want to move Toby, and you are right. If his wound breaks open, he could bleed to death. Maybe you or your deputy know how to treat such a wound. But if you don't. . . ."

He interrupted. "We got no way to keep him from bleedin' bad. My orders are to fetch him back alive."

"Stay as long as you like, Marshal. Normally the ride to Mission Dolores and back takes about four days, maybe a little less." She arose. "I hope the answer to your telegraph will tell you to allow Toby to stay at least until the wound is healed more."

As the large man arose to depart, Lillian Monteverde also said, "If I had known you sent your deputy alone, I would have sent some riders with him."

Marshal Harding's forehead creased slightly. "Why, ma'am?"

"Lately we have lost horses to Indians." She made a slight deprecatory gesture with her hands. "They have always been troublesome. My husband's grandfather gave them beef not to raid us. During my husband's lifetime Trinitaria gave them horses, too." At his direct look she faintly smiled. "Marshal, Trinitaria is large. Indians used to raid the ranch often . . . until my husband's people discovered how to stop it. Trinitaria has given them animals for many years."

"An' they left you alone?"

Lillian nodded. "Not always, but Trinitaria has been raided less than other ranches. And we have not lost people to Indians in many years."

"Are they still troublesome?"

"*¿Quien sabe?* Who knows when they will come? Not the old ones, I think, but the younger ones get restless. The *mayordomo* told me we are missing some horses lately." She shrugged. "At one time all this country was Apacheria. They don't raid as much as they used to but . . . as the *mayordomo* says, stealing horses is something they get in their mother's milk. If you had told me. . . ."

Marshal Harding crossed the yard with Lillian Monteverde watching. When he disappeared inside the barn, she turned back to the house, closed the massive door, and leaned on it. Later, she took the tray of food from the Indian woman, carried it to Toby's room, placed it upon the bedside table without looking at him and would have left the room if he hadn't said, "Ma'am?"

She turned, feeling the color come into her face. In an impersonal voice she told him about the deputy marshal riding to Dolores.

He ignored that. "Why did you do that?" he asked.

Her color remained high. She was supposed to say something that would crush his feelings but could not think of anything appropriate, so she left the room without speaking.

When Juanita Flores came to re-dress his wound, he asked questions of her about *la patrona.* She answered guardedly. By the time she was finished and ready to depart, she met his gaze head-on and said, "The *mayordomo* went with the riders this morning very early." Her statement was meant to arouse his curiosity. It didn't.

"Juanita . . . how old is *la patrona?*"

She hesitated in the doorway with her bandaging things, looking directly at him. "I don't know her age. Does it matter?"

"No. I expect it don't. Tell me something: she had no children?"

Juanita Flores was uncomfortable under his questioning. As for the latest question, she had no idea. "It was God's will," she told him and fled.

Later, with the day well along, Marshal Harding came to see Toby. As before the large man dwarfed the chair he sat on when he spoke. "I turned them two fellers loose who said you shot the wagon driver in the back." At Toby's questioning expression the large man explained. "Liars come in all sizes, Mister Lincoln. If I'd taken them north as witnesses, they'd have ended up making me look like a fool. They're a pair to draw to. For a bottle of whiskey they'd sell their mothers."

Harding got comfortable. "My problem is that I got to take you back to stand trial, an' the longer I'm down here talkin' to folks . . . includin' you . . . the more I get the feelin' no one got shot in the back, that it was as they told me in that little town. You called Bannion, give him a chance, an' killed him because you're faster with weapons than Bannion was.

"About the wagon driver I got more trouble. Most folks

who saw the fight said you shot him while he was standin' to one side of Bannion."

Toby interrupted. "I told you I didn't mean to shoot the scrawny one. You can believe me or not. I thought I aimed at Bannion. I guess Manuel was right. He said I was fast enough but couldn't shoot straight worth a damn."

"Who is Manuel?"

"The feller they call Desdentado because he has no teeth. He taught me to draw an' fire."

Marshal Harding sat silent for a while. He had met the toothless man whose smile was genuine and whose eyes twinkled. He asked why Toby had gone to Manuel Acosta to learn about drawing and firing.

"Because the *mayordomo* thought I should. He said Manuel Acosta shot it out down in Mexico with a passel of men, an' killed every man-jack among them."

"You sure it was down in Mexico an' not up here?"

"That's what I was told."

"By who?"

"The *mayordomo*. Them two been friends for years."

"I'll talk to the *mayordomo* when he comes in this evening." Boyd Harding arose, looked down, and asked a question. "How's the wound coming?"

Toby answered candidly. "Broke open a little but mainly the healin' is doin' right well."

"Glad to hear it," Harding said. "Maybe in another few days . . . when Walt gets back . . . we can load you up and head north. I expect we can rig the prison wagon with blankets an' straw."

Lillian Monteverde appeared in the doorway, big-eyed and pale. "Marshal, the riders have your deputy in the *jacal*. He has been hurt. They found him in some rocks without his horse."

The large man could move fast when he had to. He moved fast now with Lillian Monteverde following. Toby eased back, wondering. From what Lillian had said, it sounded to him as though the deputy's horse had spooked — there were rattlesnakes in the south desert — and had bucked the deputy off in some rocks.

He had no premonition. In fact, he felt relieved because with his deputy injured the big man would be delayed in his plan to take him north in the prison wagon.

Toby slept until late afternoon when Juanita Flores appeared to feed him and examine the bandaged leg. What she had to say was a total surprise to him.

"*¡Indios!* There haven't been no raiders in years. They caught the deputy in the open. They were hidden in some rocks. The *vaqueros* heard gunshots. By the time they got close, the Indians had seen their dust and ran away. They brought him back. I went to care for him, but others was already there."

Toby asked how badly he had been hurt and got the shrug he might have expected since Juanita Flores had not been able to look closely at the injured man. "I don't know how bad, but I can tell you there was bloody rags in the *jacal,* along with *vaqueros* and some women who were ringing their hands and saying their beads."

Toby ate after Juanita Flores had departed. His feelings were mixed. He had never liked the deputy marshal, and now Marshal Harding would have no help carrying Toby back up north. Most likely the injured deputy would ride inside with Toby, if the marshal decided to make the trip anyway, which was possible; but if Walt Rowe was seriously injured, Marshal Harding would be unable to leave for several days. Maybe several weeks, depending on the deputy's injuries.

The pleasant Indian woman came to light Toby's lamp.

He asked her if she knew the condition of the lawman. She smiled and shook her head. Her English was very limited in any case. After she left, Toby lay back, looking at the ceiling with its massive, age-darkened balks at spaced intervals with plastered-over adobe between the balks.

It was dark when the *mayordomo* came to consider Toby solemnly as he said, "The skinny lawman rode near some rocks where Apaches were waiting." Salazar pulled up a chair and sank down. He looked tired. "The riders heard gunshots and when they came up the Indians rode hell-for-leather. The *vaqueros* brought the hurt man back on a sling made of their saddle blankets."

"How bad off is he?" Toby asked.

Salazar answered, while gravely regarding the headboard above Toby's face. "He will live. Mostly he was cut by pieces of rock where the bullets struck." Salazar's dark eyes came lower. "He bled some, of course, but I think he was scairt bad because he was still shaking when he was put on the pallet in their hut. Something like that can make a man's nerves raw for several days."

Toby asked if *la patrona* had sent for the doctor over at Mission Dolores. Salazar arose, hat in hand, when he replied, "His wounds are not that bad, I think. Even if the doctor could come, it might not be for a week or two." The *mayordomo* went as far as the doorway before speaking again — in the same graveyard voice. "It is the first raid by Apaches in many years." He gazed impassively at Toby. "The marshal is troubled. He asked *la patrona* if any of our men could make the trip to send a telegraph up north. She told him when the Apaches are loose, no one is safe. No, she would not ask any of us to make the ride."

Chapter Seventeen

Some Answers and One Surprise

Toby heard the commotion without any idea what caused it. When the Indian woman came to bring a fresh pitcher of water, he asked her, and she replied with difficulty.

"It is an old cow with one horn. They are throwing her onto the ground to put medicine in the hole of her horn. Am I understood?"

Toby smiled. "You manage English much better than I manage Spanish."

He was dozing when Juanita Flores appeared with her bandaging material. As she worked, she told him she had given what remained of the white powder and the contents of the blue bottle to the *mayordomo* to be used on the one-horned cow.

She also quickly said, "The wound is closed. Look. It will be recovered in another few weeks and you can walk . . . I think anyway."

He leaned to look. For a fact even the two small places, which had bled when he had got into the chair, looked healed. He lay back.

"How is the lawman?"

She finished the fresh bandage as she replied. "The *mayordomo* said if Ignacio and the others hadn't come, the Indians would have killed him. He told me where the lawman was in the rocks was a poor place for defense."

Toby repeated the question: "How is he?"

Juanita Flores leaned back considering her handiwork when she replied. "No bullets hit him, but he has many wounds from sharp rock." She gathered her things and finally looked at Toby. "Old Emilia says if he is not kept clean and tranquil, he will get infected." Juanita broadly smiled and departed.

Toby had the feeling that those who visited him were not sorry for the injured lawman. Even Marshal Harding was matter-of-fact when he came after supper to visit and said he intended to go Indian-hunting in the morning, that when broncos attacked a federal lawman it would normally bring in the Army. He had been told the nearest bivouac was sixty miles southwest — at Mission Dolores, which was too far. The Indians would be out of the country by the time the Army arrived, so he would go alone.

He did not once mention his deputy, but he did say he should have gone himself; his second nature, after so many years, was just naturally to avoid places where there could be an ambush.

As he arose to depart, Toby asked him if he thought there might be an attack on the ranch. Harding pondered briefly before shaking his head.

"Nothin' big. We got 'em pretty well corralled on reservations. I expect there'll always be stronghearts who bust loose. They've had that problem up north with the Sioux an' Cheyenne."

Two days later with the deputy marshal recovering, Toby wondered about Lillian Monteverde. She had not been to see him. He speculated about the reason. Perhaps she was too embarrassed over what had happened the last time she was in his room.

The more he thought about the kiss, the more difficult

it seemed for him to find a reason for it. Things had been hectic between them before it happened. After it happened, she had fled from the room and had clearly been avoiding him since.

The evening of the third day Marshal Harding came in, sat down, and fished several spent cartridge cases from a pocket which he held out for Toby to examine. He asked if Toby knew what he saw. Toby answered curtly; everyone knew a spent bullet casing when they saw one.

Marshal Harding pocketed the casings as he spoke. "They are from a Sharps rifle, most likely a carbine. The kind of gun they give the Army ten, fifteen years ago, before they give 'em repeating guns." The large man paused before also saying. "Injuns use 'em. If you know anythin' about cartridge casings, Mister Lincoln, you seen that them casings been re-loaded many times until the casing is so worn down they can't no more put out a bullet at full range." The big man offered a wintry smile. "Maybe that's what kept my deputy from gettin' killed. He told me he didn't see no Indians when they fired on him from different places. He said he didn't see but one Indian durin' the fight, a tall, skinny bronco with a 'Pache sweatband around his forehead, and he only got a quick sightin' of that one."

Marshal Harding eased back in the chair, sober and grave. "When I'm able, I'll see that the Army's told. They'll run them bastards down and settle with 'em."

Toby asked to see the casings again. He knew nothing about re-loading bullet casings nor, for that matter, Sharps carbines or southwestern Indians.

He and the marshal hunched over the hand holding the casings. Harding eventually said, "Them damned ragheads. I've come onto them before, but not this far south. O' course, then, I've never been sent this far south before. I can tell you, Mister Lincoln, if they're off the reservation, the Army's got to be told. They'll put 'em back in short order. As many as they don't kill."

Three days later Juanita Flores came to replace the bandage and said, "The *Señora* is back . . . God be praised."

"Back from where?"

"Santa Fé."

He had very little knowledge of the territory outside of Trinitaria and Trabajo. "Where is Santa Fé?"

"It is the capital of the territory. It is where the military governor lives. I think his name is Wallace."

Toby waited impatiently for *la patrona* to visit his room, but she did not appear. The next morning, when the pleasant Indian woman brought breakfast, he asked her to tell *la patrona* he wanted to see her. Later, close to evening, he became convinced the Indian woman had not carried his message. Fifteen minutes later Lillian Monteverde appeared in the doorway. She looked fresh and handsome but, in fact, she was tired from a long trip with few places to rest.

He nodded toward the chair at bedside and asked her in Spanish to be seated. Her lips faintly quirked as she walked over and sat down. Her face was impassive when she said, "They have been teaching you. Even your accent is good." She relaxed before speaking again. "The marshal cannot take you up north to be tried."

Toby's eyes narrowed slightly. "He can't?"

"No. The governor in Santa Fé rescinded the extradition order." At his blank look, she said, "He withdrew it, canceled it. *¿Comprende?*"

He nodded. "Can he do that, ma'am?"

"Yes, and he did do it. He will send men from Santa

Fé to investigate what happened in Trabajo. He said, if I told him the truth, he will write to Denver and to Washington that you did not commit murder, that you were defending yourself." She looked straight at him.

He had to look elsewhere when he said, *"Gracias a Dios."*

She laughed. "They *have* been teaching you."

He ignored that to look at her. "I don't know how to tell you how beholden I am to you, ma'am. I wondered why you hadn't been to see me. I thought it was because . . . of that other thing."

She said nothing. For about eight days she had sought the reason for having kissed him. She was a woman without a husband, without children, with only Trinitaria. For seven years she had hardened herself to the task of managing a huge grant of land with the livestock, and its people dependent on her judgment.

She had done it well, but there was a loneliness at Trinitaria that its people could not appease. She looked steadily at him as she said, "I don't know exactly why, Toby. I was upset, we were arguing . . . I just did it."

"Ma'am." He held her gaze. "Would you be mad if I asked if I could kiss you . . . sort of return it?"

Her color climbed, but she did not look away. She leaned so he would not have to raise much from the bed. He kissed her gently. She raised both arms to his shoulders and returned the kiss, then she sank back, wide-eyed and silent.

"Toby. Do you know how old I am?"

"No, ma'am."

"Ten years older than you are."

He smiled. "You could be fifty years older. Does it matter?"

She arose from the chair. He held out a hand which

she considered before taking it. He squeezed, she squeezed back, and hurried from the room.

She did not return to his room for two days. On the second day he had another visitor, Marshal Harding, looking as solemn as an owl.

He sat down, gazing steadily at Toby. "You got a real influential friend, Mister Lincoln." He removed a folded paper from a pocket and held it out. "Gov'ner Wallace took back his agreement to extradite you to Colorado." Toby made no move to take the paper, so the marshal carefully tucked it back in a pocket. "In all my twenty-three years of marshaling I never had this happen before."

"Mister Harding, the gunfight was exactly as I told you. There was two men from Trinitaria with me. Ask them."

"I did," the marshal replied, and there was something close to a grim twinkle in his eyes. "The tall, thin man without teeth. . . ."

"Desdentado."

The marshal ignored the interruption. "He told me you are as fast with a gun as anyone . . . but the only way you'd hit a barn was if you was inside it. He said he was no more'n thirty feet when the firin' commenced. He thought sure your shot would put Bannion down. Instead it hit the feller standin' next to him. Well, Mister Lincoln, I've seen my share of gunmen an' I've seen the best of 'em miss by a yard or two." As he arose, the large man stood for a moment, looking down. "I hope your leg gets well fast." He did not move, and a long moment later he also said, "My deputy's fit to travel. Not on horseback, but he'll do fine in the prison wagon. To be right truthful with you, I'd like to get the hell out of this country, an' for a fact I won't be back.

"I been over twenty-three years at my trade. I been thinkin' about retiring for some time. Now, when I go back up north and don't have you, just the piece of paper Miz Monteverde fetched back from Santa Fé, they'll fire me for failin' to do what I was ordered to do . . . unless I quit first."

Toby liked the large man. "If it'll help, I'll come north as soon as I can travel an'. . . ."

"No need, Mister Lincoln. I own a saloon up near Canon City. I kind've like the notion of not havin' to ride hundreds of miles to find someone. I'm gettin' too old for this business."

He leaned to extend a huge paw of a hand. Toby shook it and watched the large man pass from sight beyond the doorway.

He sank back, gazing at the ceiling. How Lillian Monteverde had managed all this was a wonder. When Juanita Flores came to re-bandage the leg, she said, "You heal very fast," and leaned back to smile at him. "Three, maybe four more weeks and you can stand up."

He lowered his gaze to her face. "I need you to tell me something."

Her smile faded, replaced by an expression of wariness. "If I can."

"La patrona. . . ."

She sprang off the chair, said, "I can tell you nothing," and left the room.

Later, with the day wearing along, with thin shadows forming, Leon Salazar arrived at bedside, holding his hat in both hands when he said, "We cleaned out the hole in the one-horned cow's head. This afternoon she was quiet and gave milk to her puny calf. I think we keep her corralled for a few days to be sure the maggots don't come back, then turn her out."

Toby smiled. "Thanks. She's just an old cow, but. . . ."

"I understand," the *mayordomo* said. "Once I had a sick horse. I rode him most of the time. We did everything we could think of to make him better."

"And . . . ?" Toby asked

"He died." The *mayordomo* sat on the bedside chair, holding his hat in his lap. "I'll tell you something about men and animals: one don't live long enough or the other one lives too long. Desdentado had a dog for years. It got too old and died in its sleep. That's when Manuel drank red wine every day. His family died years ago. All he had was that old dog."

Toby had a question. He had tried it on Juanita Flores and she had fled. He tried it on the *mayordomo*. "*Jefe*, why didn't she marry again?"

He did not say whom he meant. Salazar's gaze was steady and a little hard. Juanita Flores had carried Emilia Escobar's gossip to him. Besides, there are always little signs.

"I don't know, but I can tell you running Trinitaria is a full-time job. Even more than a full-time job. Trinitaria has been her husband, but that is not natural. I know." Salazar made a little wintry smile. "I can tell you . . . in this life we only think we are the masters. We're not. There is something . . . whatever it is . . . that plans for things to happen, and we do them. *¿Comprende?*"

Toby did not comprehend, nor was he interested in abstractions; he was interested in the subject toward which he again guided their conversation. "She should have re-married, *jefe*."

The *mayordomo* shrugged, sighed, and arose from the chair. All this talk about *la patrona* made him uncomfortable. "The *gringo* lawman borrowed a wagon to take his deputy to Trabajo. From there he will go back where he came from, driving the prison wagon."

Toby nodded. "Did *la patrona* tell you why they left?"

La Señora again! Salazar shook his head, mumbled something about getting well, and departed.

It was not quite dusk when Lillian Monteverde arrived with a basin of water and the straight razor. She was not wearing black. Her hair shone like a raven's wing except at the temples. Her features, like her complexion, were perfect.

He smiled and she smiled back, but not until she had shaved him, washed his face afterwards, and was preparing to leave did either of them speak. It was Toby. He said, "Juanita Flores says I can walk in a few weeks. If I can walk, I can ride."

She sat down with the basin and its contents in her lap. "Ride . . . where?"

"Nowhere, ma'am. Unless you don't need a *gringo vaquero.*"

She relaxed, pointed to clothing in a corner, and said, "You don't know if they will fit."

He knew who had got the boots and clothing and he was grateful. In time he would give proper thanks to Desdentado and the *jefe,* but the clothing had nothing to do with what he had said to her. He tried one more time.

"Ma'am, somewhere there is another Trinitaria?"

Her gaze did not waver. "Yes, there must be. New Mexico territory is very large. Do you want to find another Trinitaria, Toby?"

He had an abrupt surge of impatience. This was like playing cards — his move, then someone else's move, then his move again.

"There ain't another Trinitaria. There ain't another

bunch of folks like the ones right here."

"Then stay," she told him, and he stated the question she was dreading to hear.

"Ma'am, do *you* want me to stay?"

She did not have to answer. The Indian woman appeared in the doorway, twisting her apron in both hands. "*Señora . . .* ?"

Lillian arose holding the basin. "*Dorotea . . .* ?"

"*¡Soldados, Señora!*"

Lillian left without even looking back, with the Indian woman following.

Toby shoved up into a full sitting position. Both women had been upset. Something was happening and he incorrectly assumed he was the cause of it because he had been the only cause of the disruption of everything since the shooting.

He swore and moved his injured leg warily. There was no pain but neither was there a good response, which meant that, even if he got out of the bed, he probably could not move without stumbling or falling because the leg simply would not do what legs were supposed to do.

He had a little bell on the bedside table which he rarely used. He considered using it now, but instinct told him it would be wasted effort. Whatever was happening elsewhere, he was separated from it. At least for the time being.

He did get out of the bed, limped as far as the dresser where the new clothing and boots were, wondered more about the boots fitting than the trousers and shirt, and might have tried the boots but a calm male voice spoke from the doorway.

"Aha, *compañero!* Why are you away from the bed?"

Ignacio was in the doorway. Toby reddened, feeling like a little boy caught in a misdemeanor. He got back to the bed and sat on it. He tried to arrange words Ignacio would understand. "*¿Qué hay?* What is happening?"

The *vaquero* spread his arms, palms down. "*Soldados* . . . soldiers. Given to going with a little flag."

"Soldiers in the yard, Ignacio?"

"Yes. In the yard, soldiers."

"What do they want?" Toby asked, and the unflappable *vaquero* smiled before replying. "To me I am not told. Only to *la patrona* an' *el jefe.* I am here because it was told to me to visit you."

"Visit me, why?"

This was about to overwhelm Ignacio, so all he gave for an answer was something Toby had become accustomed to — a shrug, went to the bedside chair, and sat down smiling.

He hadn't been told by the *mayordomo* to visit; he had been told by the *mayordomo* to stay with Toby, not to allow anyone, even all the soldiers in the yard, to take Toby from his room.

Chapter Eighteen

Full Circle

It was evening before the *mayordomo* appeared in Toby's doorway to dismiss Ignacio, who left with a smile and a wicked wink at Toby.

The *mayordomo* sank down on the bedside chair, hat in hand, and ruefully said, "*La patrona* said for me to tell you it is now all right."

"What in hell is all right, *jefe?*"

"The soldiers are gone. They were making one of their routine sweeps through the reservation. They make a head count now and then."

"An' they come up missin' some raiders?"

Salazar shook his head.

"No. They told *La Señora* there was no missing Indians."

Toby faintly frowned.

"They must not have made much of a head count, *jefe*. What about the Indians that tried to kill that deputy marshal?"

"*La patrona* did not mention that. Neither did I. The officer was pleasant but refused *la patrona*'s offer for him an' his soldiers to spend the night in the yard." Salazar wryly smiled. "It is the custom. One must be hospitable even to *soldados gringos*."

"*Jefe,* why didn't you tell the soldiers about the Indian

attack on that lawman?"

"Why should that be mentioned? The deputy survived. I don't know what happened to his horse. Maybe the Indians got it." Salazar abruptly arose. This time he did smile. "The officer said they made a head count. No Indians was off the reservation." Salazar shrugged. "It would not be right to say we knew better, that raiders had been off the reservation, would it? Say something like that to an officer of the Army . . . call him a liar? No, *compañero,* that would be very bad manners."

After the *mayordomo* departed, Toby stared at the far wall for a long time. He thought he was beginning to understand these people, along with learning their language — but what the *mayordomo* had told him! The soldiers should have been told, if for no other reason than so they would make a point of warning others as they traveled through the countryside.

Juanita Flores brought his supper and sat at bedside. She liked company; she also liked to talk. And he was handsome — for a *gringo.* Handsome and possessed of a good heart. But he was young; sometimes young men saddled up and rode away. Older men, like the *mayordomo,* were likely to be more settled, more permanent in their lives.

She told him *la patrona* and Salazar had met with the soldiers. She only knew what had transpired from the *mayordomo,* so what she said Toby already knew. But it bothered him that the attack on the deputy marshal had been withheld.

He said, "Them Indians will likely attack other people."

Juanita Flores neither agreed nor disagreed; instead she said, "The *mayordomo* said when they ran away, they went in the direction of the reservation."

Toby scowled.

"Juanita, that's the same direction them soldiers took to get here."

"Well, but *los indios* are very *coyote.* They would see soldiers and hide from them."

The discussion might have continued but for the arrival of *la patrona.* Juanita departed, leaving the tray of food behind. It had not been touched.

Lillian Monteverde sat on the vacated chair.

"You aren't hungry?" she asked.

Toby had forgotten the tray.

"Why didn't you tell the soldiers about them Apaches ambushin' the deputy marshal, ma'am?"

"There was no reason, Toby. They were on their way back to Mission Dolores. They had been riding a long time . . . and . . . if they went after the Indians, the trail was cold."

"But ma'am, bronco Indians out raidin' could attack other places."

She answered that serenely.

"If they had, by now we would have heard. The marshal and his deputy are on their way back where they came from. What happened was one of those things we live with in this country, but it has happened less as time passes. Why don't you eat?"

He considered the tray, then looked at her and told the truth when he said, "With you settin' there I don't have no appetite."

She did not smile. "Toby . . . ?"

"Yes, ma'am?"

"Toby . . . don't call me ma'am."

"What should I call you?"

She bewildered him by what she now did. As she had done before, she arose and left the room.

He did not eat until it was dark with a soft breeze

coming from the north.

One week later he got out of bed, put on the new clothes, got as far as tugging on the boots, and got no further. When he tugged, his leg hurt. He sat on a chair fully dressed, except for one boot. He was still sitting like that when *la patrona* came to shave him, and stopped in her tracks. He sheepishly grinned.

"I guess not quite yet," he told her, hobbled back to the bed, and lay out full length fully clothed except for one boot.

She propped him up, lathered his face — across the mouth again — and whetted the razor with sure, long even strokes. She said, "Turn your head to the right, please. Fine. Toby, don't do that again. Your leg isn't ready. I know what impatience is, but re-opening the wound will keep you in bed until Christmas."

She shaved his upper lip and chin last. When she toweled his face with the warm, wet towel, he finally could speak.

"Ma'am, I don't much like livin' off you an' givin' nothin' in return."

She put the shaving things aside and sat on the bedside chair.

"You will be here at Christmas time anyway. Unless you have changed your mind about staying."

The idea of leaving Trinitaria had not entered his mind since the last time this topic came up between them.

"I'll be here at Christmas time, but I'm runnin' up a hell of a tab, ma'am."

She considered him over a long space of silence before saying, "You owe Trinitaria nothing. We have always taken care of our own. You are one of us. The men like you. Juanita Flores told me she thinks you are handsome . . . for a *gringo*."

He was quiet for a long time. Lillian Monteverde was a wise and knowledgeable woman. She did not break the silence until he turned to look at her, then she faintly smiled.

"I am too old, Toby. In ten years I will be forty. Among my people that is very old."

He reddened. "In ten years I'll be a tad over thirty . . . that's old too, isn't it?"

She knew about arguing with him.

"If you think it is, then it must be. What I am saying is that. . . . This is very difficult, Toby."

He could have agreed with her, but instead he smiled. "Ma'am, you're prettier'n a speckled bird."

She laughed, gently wagged her head, considered the things that stood between them, and said, "Would you like to go buggy riding with me tomorrow?"

"Yes'm, I would for a fact."

"Don't put on that boot. I'll have someone bring you a moccasin." She arose with high color and very bright dark eyes. "Sleep well. Good night."

After she left the room, he snorted. Sleep well!

In her own room Lillian Monteverde sat before a dressing table flanked by two candles, brushing her hair and avoiding the eyes looking back from the mirror. She was not a woman given to recklessness or boldness but, as God knew, the heart had many facets and occasionally, although of a certainty not often, a shadow obscured one of those facets, and when that rarity occurred, the heart spoke instead of the mind.

The following morning she had a light top-buggy readied behind a big seal brown mare with the disposition of a four-legged saint. She asked the *mayordomo* to go to the main house and assist Toby to cross the yard. Salazar obeyed to the letter, his leathery, lined face as impassive as stone.

When they left the yard with the first high haze which usually presaged autumn on the desert, and less heat than there had been for months, people watched from doorways and from beneath overhead *ramadas*. Juanita Flores addressed the old woman standing with her.

"It is possible, Emilia, that having a man in her house after so many years of not having one. . . ."

The old woman interrupted, squinting out where the buggy was getting small.

"It would depend on the man, would it not? This one is young but . . . he saved *Tía* Maria, and he worried about that crazy old cow, and other things. I think *la señora* is ready. I think God in His wisdom sent her a good man, maybe just in time."

"Just in time, Emilia?"

"Well, she gets no younger. Another few years of having no man and of a certainty she would become shriveled of the mind and body."

Juanita Flores went to the *jacal* of the *mayordomo*. She stopped just short of entering when she heard a voice she instantly recognized say, "This wine is getting sour, *jefe*. How many of those Indian guns did you have?"

"I told you, twelve from fights when *el patrón* was alive. Twelve of the old Sharps carbines and six bandoleers off corpses. And why, may I ask, did you have to stand up where the deputy marshal could see you?"

"Because his pistol would not reach that far."

"But he might have recognized you."

Desdentado made a scornful sound. "He had to think it was an Apache, didn't he? I only jumped up once, then dropped down. What worried me, *jefe*, was those old guns and that the shortened casings might hit the man."

"Well it didn't happen, did it?"

Desdentado waited until he had emptied the tin cup to reply. "No, but even aiming at the rocks, not at the man, with weapons like that, a man could not be certain. Tell me, *jefe,* was it your idea or *la patrona*'s?"

The *mayordomo* abruptly arose from the table.

"There is someone outside."

As he went to the door Manuel Acosta said, "There is always someone outside," and refilled his tin cup.

The mayordomo returned, sat down, and reached for his cup.

"Nada," he grumbled as Desdentado got to his feet. "A *fantasma, viejo, adios."*

Juanita Flores peeked from behind the house, waited until the tall, thin man was almost to his own residence, then smoothed her skirt, took down a deep breath and entered the *jacal* wearing a wide, false smile.

The *mayordomo* looked up at her and spoke in a challenging tone.

"I am having some wine."

She moved close, placed a hand on his shoulder, leaned and kissed his unshaven cheek. "For me to prepare a meal will take time. Re-fill the cup."

He didn't refill the cup. He was already bothered by a shadowy vision and an inexplicable warmth of the body.

Lillian Monteverde and Toby Lincoln were married after Christmas in the little white-washed chapel Toby had once thought was a granary. The priest came from Mission Dolores.

They had four children. The first was a boy and he was named Abel. The girls were named — first — Buttercup. The second girl was named Molly for the big woman who'd had a cafe in a town which no longer existed. Their last and youngest child was a boy. He was named Buttons.

Had *la patrona* conceived the idea of delaying the federal lawmen by having *vaqueros,* pretending to be Apaches, ambush the deputy marshal? *¿Quien sabe?* Who knows? But of a certainty, there was the desired delay.

Lauran Paine who, under his own name and various pseudonyms has written over 900 books, was born in Duluth, Minnesota, a descendant of the Revolutionary War patriot and author, Thomas Paine. His family moved to California when he was at an early age and his apprenticeship as a Western writer came about through the years he spent in the livestock trade, rodeos, and even motion pictures where he served as an extra because of his expert horsemanship in several films starring movie cowboy Johnny Mack Brown. In the late 1930s, Paine trapped wild horses in northern Arizona and even, for a time, worked as a professional farrier. Paine came to know the Old West through the eyes of many who had been born in the previous century and he learned that Western life had been very different from the way it was portrayed on the screen. "I knew men who had killed other men," he later recalled. "But they were the exceptions. Prior to and during the Depression, people were just too busy eking out an existence to indulge in Saturday-night brawls." He served in the U.S. Navy in the Second World War and began writing for Western pulp magazines following his discharge. It is interesting to note that all of his earliest novels (written under his own name and the pseudonym Mark Carrel) were published in the British market and he soon had as strong a following in that country as in the United States. Paine's Western fiction is characterized by strong plots, authenticity, an apparently effortless ability to construct situation and character, and a preference for building his stories upon a solid foundation of historical fact. ADOBE EMPIRE (1956), one of his best novels, is a fictionalized account of the last twenty years in the life of trader William Bent and, in an off-trail way, has a melancholy, bittersweet texture that is not easily forgotten. MOON PRAIRIE (1950), first published in the United States in 1994, is a memorable story set during the mountain man period of the frontier. In later novels such as THE HOMESTEADERS (1986) or THE OPEN RANGE MEN (1990), he showed that the special magic and power of his stories and characters had only matured along with his basic themes of changing times, changing attitudes, learning from experience, respecting nature, and the yearning for a simpler, more moderate way of life. His fine Western stories will be regularly appearing as Five Star Westerns.